Jessica
Faeries Wear Boots
An After Dark Novella

Megan Slayer

Jessica: Faeries Wear Boots – An After Dark Novella
Copyright © 2019, Wendi Zwaduk
Print Cover by BigZDesigns
Published by Megan Slayer Publications
2019

Warning: All rights reserved. The unauthorized reproduction or distribution of this copyrighted work is illegal. Criminal copyright infringement, including infringement without monetary gain, is investigated by the FBI and is punishable by up to 5 years in federal prison and a fine of $250,000.

Electronic Release: June 2019
Print Release Summer 2019

This is a work of fiction. Names, characters, places and occurrences are a product of the author's imagination. Any resemblance to actual persons, living or dead, places or occurrences, is purely coincidental.

DEDICATION

For my Lucky Ducks. I write because of you.
For Kris because you keep putting up with me. You rock.
For JPZ. You know why.

Trademark: Converse

CONTENTS

Chapter One	1
Chapter Two	17
Chapter Three	34
Chapter Four	54
Chapter Five	71
Chapter Six	85
About the Author	109
After Dark Titles	111

Can a faerie running from trouble and a demon full of it make love work?

Jessica's never been the favorite faerie in the family. She's rough around the edges and runs with a dangerous crowd. She wants to be loved, but who wants the daughter of the head faerie? She's got secrets that could be deal breakers. Guys don't want to date faeries and she's tired of dead ends. Isn't there one good man interested in being with a dark faerie?

Although Lane plays a mage on television, it's just a role. No one cares that he's a demon — not even Jessica. He senses the darkness within her, but there's something else. She's not like the others he's met before. He wants to save her, even if only from herself. Will she accept the love of a demon, or run away before he has a chance to prove he's worthy of a faerie?

CHAPTER ONE

"I want to stretch my wings with someone who loves me." Jessica snorted as she removed her jacket. Coming to the comic convention had been a stroke of genius. She could stretch her wings and no one would care. They'd think she was cosplaying. Good. Let them. Her wings were part of her, but looked no different than some of the well-crafted costumes. Their wings would come off at the end of the day. Hers would bleed if clipped.

But for the moment, she was free and hiding in plain sight. Her concerns didn't bother her. Let the shit in her life come crashing down after she left the convention hall. For the next couple hours, she was just another cosplayer. No one would know she was a real faerie or that she could do magic. They'd think she was someone wrapped up in making her wings look as realistic as possible. Her mother couldn't look down on her for a few moments and the paranormals weren't going to ignore her. She wasn't Hestia's daughter or Cordelia's cousin—she could be herself. She sensed other paranormals around, but if they weren't going to point her out, she'd keep her mouth shut about them, too.

She draped her jacket over her arm and strolled the aisles of the convention. Pop-up shops offered almost any comic book wanted, knickknacks created to commemorate comic book characters, T-shirts, artwork and more. She passed a couple of the artists drawing characters while people waited. A few authors were sprinkled in for good measure.

When she turned the corner to the middle aisle, she noticed the banners emblazoned with names of people she'd never heard of, but lots more people were in lines beneath the banners. She recognized one of the names, but had no desire to meet the actor.

"May I take a photo with you and those wings?" a girl asked. "They're the best I've seen so far."

Jess shrugged. "Sure." She popped a pose, then offered a sly grin.

The girl snapped the picture with her phone, then tucked the phone away. "Do you always wear leather with your wings? I get too hot when I wear only black." She frowned. "I love the green in your hair. What product do you use to get that color?"

"I buy a box of color at the store. The one for dark hair." Jessica clutched her jacket. "As for the leather, I work at night and it's cooler, so I like to stay warm."

"I love your boots." The girl paused. "I

know you, don't I? Aren't you in the show *Story Book*?"

"No." She'd never heard of any television show called *Story Book*. "Sorry. I'm not famous." Not in the least.

"You look like you should be on that show. Like you're someone famous, but going under the radar." She shrugged. "Oh well. Thanks for the picture."

"No sweat." Jessica waved. "See you." She kept making her way down the aisle. The interaction with the girl stayed in her mind. What an odd thing, someone thinking she was famous. Working in a bar wasn't her idea of fame. Hell, she spent more time mopping up after drunks than she did much else. Most people wanted her to listen to their problems and be their therapist. No one cared what she thought or if she even wanted to hear their complaints. She'd almost forgot what having a friend was like. Lando, the other bartender and the one paranormal who hadn't tried to make a move on her, wasn't her friend — more like the scary guy who ruled the bar and hit on the guys she liked.

She laced her fingers together beneath her jacket and continued to stroll. A sign directed attendees to the smaller presentations and speakers. One placard mentioned a Q & A with a mage.

She snorted. The last mage she knew wanted to con folks out of money. She doubted this was the same guy, who anything was possible. Still, it intrigued her. She wandered into the room. People milled about the space and a few sat in chairs in the front row.

What the hell? Why not listen to the guy? He probably wasn't a mage, but she doubted anyone in the room cared. They wanted to see the guy. Maybe he'd be handsome and good eye candy. She sat in the last row on the aisle. The projector turned on, emblazoning the wall with the name of the presenter.

Lane Michaels

She tucked her wings away and propped her feet on the empty chair in front of her.

"Are you a Michaels Maniac?" a woman in a purple cloak asked. She held up buttons. "You need this."

"What's it do?" The last time someone gave her a random object, Jessica lost feeling in her fingertips and the glitter fell off her wings for a week. She'd rather know the effects instead of feeling them.

"It's a button to signify you're a fan of Lane." She offered Jessica the button again. "I buy them and give one to each member of his fan club."

"Oh, then don't bother. I'm not a member. I'm just nosy." Jessica smiled. "Thanks, though."

"Want to be a member?"

Jessica crooked her eyebrow. "For a small fee of twenty-nine ninety-five?"

"It's free."

"Thanks, but I'm good. I don't know who Lane is." Jessica shrugged. Her senses tingled. The woman wasn't just a fan in a purple get-up. She had demon in her. Time to shut this down before the woman did something foolish. "Guess I'm a lookie-loo," Jessica said. "No biggie. If this is for his fan club, I'll go."

"When you see him, you'll fall head over heels."

"Sure." *Not.* "Thanks, though."

"Take it. If he caught you with his gaze and you wandered in, then you're an honorary member." The woman placed the button on Jessica's lap. "Consider yourself lucky."

Jessica debated correcting her, but didn't bother. She didn't touch the button, either. Once the woman left, Jessica flicked her fingers to produce a hanky. She nestled the hanky around the button, then tucked the objects in her pocket.

Moments after the woman walked away, the announcer broke the din of conversation. He read through Lane Michaels's list of accomplishments and shows he'd starred in. Once the announcer finished, Lane Michaels emerged from behind a curtain on the right side of the room.

Jessica frowned. The tall, blond-haired man wearing sunglasses strode across the room to the platform. The camera zoomed in on him as he pulled the chair away from the table. The hoodie and leather jacket hid his frame, but the jeans encased his legs like a second skin. The white tips of his Converse shimmered. His brown eyes sparkled as he discussed his television work, then film roles. Dark roots showed in his hair. He'd been weathered — like he'd seen quite a bit in his years. He needed a shave, too.

Although he seemed nice enough, Jessica wasn't impressed. What was the draw? He had pretty eyes? So did a lot of people. He wore the leather jacket well? Big deal. He wasn't memorable.

To be honest, he looked a little rough around the edges.

"Do we have questions from the audience?" the emcee asked. "I'm sure we do."

A line of people formed at the microphone. Most of the attendees asked about television shows yet to air, movie endings no one knew about yet and two women asked for hugs.

Jessica folded her arms. For him being an actor, no one asked anything hard. He wasn't going to give away the ending to yet-to-be-released movies or shows that weren't in production. Why not ask him something interesting...like about him being a mage? Did no one care? Not even the woman in the robe?

Jessica left her chair and joined the line. She might as well ask something of substance. She stepped up to the microphone when her turn came.

"Hi," the emcee said. "What's your question?"

"Hi." Jessica adjusted the microphone. "I'd like to know how you get into character to play a mage. Isn't it hard to fake magic and remember all of those gibberish phrases?"

Lane stared at her. "Well, yeah, I have to practice the spells. I can't always get them right quickly. I've even had to write them out phonetically to make them easier to remember."

"Thank you," the emcee said.

"But he didn't answer my question." Jessica remained at the mic. With no one behind her, why give this guy an inch? "How do you get into character?"

"I put the clothes on first. That helps. Then I

deepen my voice. It fries my vocal chords, but the mage isn't me, so I don't give it thought," Lane said. "Then I read the spells and try to put myself into my character's shoes. How would he deal with situations? I've talked with people who dabble in witchcraft, too."

"Ah. Thanks." She wasn't buying his load of bullshit. If he were really into magic, he'd have more details. All he had was a couple dozen swooning women. She returned to her seat. He might be handsome, but he was lousy at telling his personal stories. She waited for the end of the chat, then left.

A woman stopped her. "You have a button."

A dull ache formed behind Jessica's eyes. "How do you know?" She'd tucked the object into her pocket. "Do you want it? I'm not part of the club."

"No, I have one." She grinned. Her robe resembled the one the first woman wore. "That button entitles you to a photo with Lane."

"Nah. I'm good." She detected demon on this woman, too. What was it with this guy? He drew demons? Or he'd fucked with the wrong magic and summoned demons. His problem—not hers.

"You get the skip the line. It's a hundred-dollar value." The woman nodded. "You'll want to. He's fun."

"A hundred dollars to get a photo with *him*?" Jesus. She might as well get into the racket. She'd take a cool hundred for a photo. Maybe she could say, photo with a real faerie...people might buy in. "Are you serious?"

"Yes. It's a great deal. Plus, he's sexy." She nudged Jessica. "Love the wings. Did you make them?"

"No." She wasn't lying. Her thoughts turned to Lane. He might be considered sexy by some.

"Who made them? There are a couple of great fabricators here." She touched one of Jessica's wings along the leading edge.

The sting of demon shot to Jessica's heart. She winced. "Nature made, I guess." She hated elaborating on the truth. "Alice Nature." The answer was her go-to, but it sounded hollow in her ears. That, or the demon's zap misfired in her brain.

"I need her number. I want a set," the woman said. "Lane will love them."

"Right. I should go." Jessica strolled away, hoping to put space between her and the woman. Although Lane intrigued her, the sting of the demon, plus the odd look from the chick in the robe unnerved her. She wasn't interested in cutting the autograph line or if Lane liked wings. He'd think they were cosplay wings anyway.

But it might be fun to dick with the guy and play the role of someone who liked him. She'd get to touch a handsome man and see if he was just as hot up close as far away. What would it hurt?

* * * *

Lane posed for yet another photo and hugged a fan. He wished the woman from the session earlier would show up. From the moment he spotted her, he was attracted. Something about her called to him and his demon liked her, too. Her questions intrigued him and he detected faerie in her. She hadn't asked about the storylines from his television shows or his personal life. She wanted to know about his craft. He hadn't run into many women who asked those kinds of questions.

Caroline, one of his assistants, paused the short line and put the barricade up. "We need to talk. I saw her."

"Did you talk to her?" He needed to connect with the mystery faerie. She wasn't like other women and that drew him in more. The producers of his show would flip out if they knew he had a real paranormal in attendance. Then again, they'd die if they knew he was a damn demon.

If he managed to get the faerie into his life, he'd never expose her to the shit he'd dealt with in California.

"Let the rest of the fans through. I hate to keep them waiting." He gestured to the barricade. "Come on."

Caroline moved the rope, but stayed beside him. "I told her about the fan club and she didn't buy it." She turned her back to the fan and fiddled with the navy curtain. "She isn't falling over to see you."

"I know." Women tended to offer themselves up to him without question—and that was before they knew he was a demon. Too many of them just wanted to be with someone famous. "Don't quit."

"I won't. I sent Elaine to work her magic, too," Caroline said.

He cringed. Magic. What bullshit. Magic

didn't exist in his world. Demons used curses and threats. But the glitter and desire from a faerie could save his humanity. Maybe. He'd sunk so low, there probably wasn't a way out.

Caroline sighed and crinkled her brow. "She'll make you human again. I know it."

"Maybe." His assistant might seem to care about him, but he doubted her authenticity. Caroline and Elaine wanted to be free again, too.

"Give us a chance," Caroline said. "You'll like her and we'll get her here."

"Sure. Now let me finish with the fans." Lane continued to pose for photos and signed autographs. His thoughts never wandered far from the faerie. Not only did she possess real magic, but she was sexy. He liked the leather and brooding style. Women in boots were a turn-on, too. Besides, if he could tell she was a faerie, she'd figure out he was a demon. If she still wanted to be around him, then great. If not, he wasn't out much.

Right?

Then why did this feel like something important? Like she was a woman he'd never forget?

Caroline returned once the last fan made her way through the line. Although Caroline left the barricade down, she turned her back to the empty strip of carpet. "Elaine found her. The perks seem to have gotten to her."

"Or she figured me out and wants to see a freak." He'd believe Elaine when he saw the faerie in front of him.

"You're not a freak," Caroline snapped. "Shut up. Here's Elaine."

Elaine strode up to him. "I did it."

"Oh?" He neatened his stack of publicity photos. "I don't see anyone." He tamped down his irritation. "Just stop acting so pushy in front of the fans. If they get a whiff of me being difficult or not acting like Magnar, it'll ruin my image."

"You worry too much," Elaine said. "She's in line and coming this way. I asked her about her wings and she said Alice Nature. What a crock. Doesn't she know I know better?"

"Enough." The faerie might have lied, but it wasn't Elaine or Caroline's job to expose the façade. "Would you want someone to know you're a damn demon?"

"No," Elaine muttered.

Caroline glared at him. "Just seal the deal."

He'd get right on it. The chemistry between him and the faerie might not be so strong up close. She might hate him.

"She's coming," Elaine said. "Don't screw this up. We need this."

"Sure." Except their motivations weren't pure. Lane leaned on the table and fiddled with his marker. At some conventions, anyone walking by could see him as he signed autographs. Not this one. Without Caroline and Elaine as his spies, he had no idea of anyone was in line.

The woman with the dazzling streak of green in her raven-colored hair, leather duds and badass wings emerged from behind the divider. The faerie.

"Hello." He offered his most-winning smile. "You're one of my fan club members."

She rolled her eyes. The heavy makeup

might not have worked on other women, but suited her well. "No, I'm not. I don't have the button where anyone can see it." She met his gaze. "Demon."

Shit. She'd figured him out. "Well...okay."

"I knew you weren't a mage. You're not even a good actor." She shook her head. "What do you want? You've pushed pretty hard to get me here. Your minions aren't exactly cunning."

"You wound me." She had him pegged so hard. Why did he like it so much? The more time he spent around her, the more he wanted to stay with her.

"See? That's how I know you're a demon. A mage wouldn't be so foolish to stroll in public or be in front of a camera. You love the attention." She cocked her hip. "Tell me I'm wrong."

"Baby, faeries don't go public either," he said. "Not in full regalia." If she wanted to challenge him, he'd give her hell, too.

She narrowed her eyes. "Alice Nature made the fucking wings."

"Does Hestia know you don't take credit for your accessories?" he asked. If he pushed her much harder, she'd probably deck him and he'd deserve it.

"My life is my own business." She notched her chin. "Demon. How do you do it? Don't you realize that if I can figure out what you really are, then others can, too? You're playing with fire. Hasn't anyone else approached you?"

He shrugged. "They have, but none cared to get to know me so well to realize I'm a demon." He wasn't sure what to do. The intention was to entice her, not turn over control and certainly not to out himself in public. But the more he looked into her dark eyes, the more he wanted to kiss her. To hell with the plan. She wasn't going to restore his humanity. She'd be the death of him. He focused on her. "All I have to do is wear my sunglasses and act unaffected. No one bothers me."

"You're crazy. Look, there's a bounty on your head. There's one on mine, too. Your minions should look out—even if they are annoying." The faerie tucked her wings away, then donned her jacket. "Alphonse Nicco is trying to capture paranormals to put in his freak show. The only trouble? No one ever makes it to the show. They mysteriously die beforehand."

"Why are you telling me this?" He already knew about Nicco and had evaded him so far. "If he's after you, then why are you here? Get out while you can."

"This, other than my job at the bar, is the safest place. Anyone could be a paranormal here." She leaned in close to him. "You're the one on television. I'm just a freak behind a bar." She crooked her brow. "Just be advised you're being watched." She left without bothering to pose for a photo or taking an autographed card.

"Wait." He caught up to her in the maze of dividers. "I'm Lane. I'm a demon, just like you figured. I'm not afraid of Nicco, but I am of you." Afraid and turned on.

"Lucky me."
"Can I call you?"
"After what I told you? No."
Shit. "Would you call me?"

"No."

He didn't want to use his demonic power on her, but he wasn't ready for her to leave. "Please? Most fans want to know my shoe size or if I'm dating someone. They don't ask tough questions and don't care about me as a person."

"So?"

"You do."

She shrugged and said nothing.

"We're allies and you feel it, too. If you didn't, you wouldn't have warned me." She had to know they were thrust into each other's orbit for a reason. Because of Nicco? He wasn't sure.

"You're not convincing me to give up my digits," she said. "I'm starting to think you're goofy."

He scrawled his phone number on his publicity photo. "Here. You take mine. Call me. If nothing else, do it to tell me you're all right and that Nicco hasn't killed you." He wanted to protect her, but demons weren't protectors. They tormented.

She folded the photo into quarters, then tucked it into her back pocket. "You're one strange demon."

"Because I'm not biting your head off? Cursing you? Throwing you into the pits of Hell?" he asked. "Or something else I missed?"

"Because you're not expecting me to jump into bed with you—yet—and you're acting human. I still expect you to try to kill me or cast me into Hades, but not here. It's too public," she said. "Besides, you don't know my name."

"I can be scary if you'd like, but I don't kill

unless I have to and no, I don't. Mine's Lane." He held out his hand. "It's nice to meet you...?"

"Jessica." She shook hands with him, then recoiled. "You're steaming."

"It's part of being a demon." His fingers tingled from her touch. He wanted more. "I promise not to cast you anywhere you don't want to go."

"Right." She turned on her heel and left.

He stared at the vacant space where she'd been and shook his head. His radar was never wrong. The chemistry between them was strong. He knew it. Why didn't she? When she held the microphone, his cock stood at attention. The sound of her voice made his heart beat faster. Her comments got him rock hard. Then there was her body—curves where a woman should be curvy, tits big enough for his hands and that ass... Christ, he wanted to gaze into her dark eyes and hold her. She captivated him like no other.

"You didn't work on her hard enough," Caroline snapped.

"You blew it," Elaine added. "We'll be stuck like this forever."

"I've been a demon for a hundred years, girls. You're lucky." Lane tossed the publicity photos onto the table and folded his arms. He debated his choices. He could stalk the faerie, but that would be too weird. She'd said she worked at a bar. What if he showed up at the establishment? He could say he'd heard about the place and needed to see it for himself.

He'd rather she'd call him because he wanted to hear her voice again. Given the chance, he'd love to hold her. He'd strip her down and taste every inch of her body.

Power surged within him. Maybe she couldn't save his soul, but she'd brought his dormant soul back to life and he wasn't ready to quit. Was it possible he'd found his soulmate?

CHAPTER TWO

Jessica left the convention center and headed to the portal beneath the transit station. She loved being able to use the portals again. Since Cory and Kali proved faeries weren't dangerous and Caden saved Ari from the ancients, magic was allowed again—except if the use drew Nicco's attention.

Fuck him. She wanted to get out of there.

Her phone buzzed as she opened the portal. She stepped through, but before she answered the call, she ensured the portal had closed. The demon crossed her mind. What if Lane followed her? She didn't want to get sloppy and entice him.

She glanced at the phone screen, then pressed the phone to her ear. "Hi Cory." She sat on the steps in her mother's basement. "What's up? Any word on Nicco?"

"I don't know anything new on Nicco, but you're in trouble," Cordelia said. "Honey, you were spotted with your wings. We're allowed to use magic, but we're supposed to keep it hushed."

"I had my wings out because I was at the comic convention where everyone is dressed in costumes," she said. "I didn't stick out. Why? Did Nicco spot me? I didn't sense him." All she'd sensed were the demons she'd dealt with—Lane and company.

"You were seen with a demon. What if he's working for Nicco?"

"I thought of that." She snorted. "He wasn't." But fucking balls. If Cory thought she might have gotten mixed up with a demon in cahoots with Nicco…then she'd really screwed up.

"How do you know?"

"Cory, relax. You worked at a public restaurant and skated the lines of behaving. Then you worked at the college and everyone called you a faerie because of your hair. No one made a big deal about it. Kali works at that refuge and Ari's writing books. What's so wrong about cutting loose every so often? We can't hide forever—not even from Nicco." Her stomach churned. She'd had enough of running from him. If he wanted to do her harm, then the old bastard could come to the house and speak to her. But her dear old dad wasn't interested. He'd rather terrorize.

"Jess…the demon wants to get close to you and if he's not lying, then he might lead Nicco right to the house," Cory said.

"Then let him. The demon I met is an actor. He's not working for Nicco—I know because I sensed it on him." She left the steps and opened a second portal to the Sidecar Bar. She entered the basement of the establishment. "I'll be okay."

Smoke from upstairs wafted down to her. Her boots caught on the stickiness on the floor. When was the last time her co-worker, Lando, mopped? She hated the drunken fights and the dankness. One day she'd break free. "I'm not anyone exciting, so even if the demon was tracking me, he's not interested in me. If he were working for Nicco, he'd have tried harder to follow me."

"You don't know you're not exciting. I thought Liam would never date me. I'm too loud and ornery," Cory said. "But he saw past that and how it all made me who I am. He and I care about you, too. You're not nobody."

"You're gorgeous and he'd have been silly not have snapped you up," Jessica said. She abandoned her jacket on her hook, then leaned against the railing. She admired Cory's ability to stay true to herself and to be approachable. She was fun. Jessica was a deterrent. When she came around, she was expected to cause trouble in bad ways. "Don't try to use your magic on me. Love ain't looking for me. Hell, I've probably got at least two women who'd like to have me killed because they think I slept with their respective boyfriends. I didn't, but no one believes me."

"I believe you," Cory said. "They're wrong and any man would be lucky to be with you. But demons don't have pure reasons for wanting anyone. He'll desire to use your magic to save his ass. It'll heal him ad he's probably got followers who want you, too."

Jessica sighed. She hated how perceptive Cory could be. That didn't mean she was ready to give up her secrets. "Do you have a harem of men who want to be with me? Or do you know where I can get a harem of men to wait on me? I want one." The men who tended to show interest in her weren't the ones she wanted to be with. Drunks weren't her idea of fun. Between her style choices, her living situation and her faerie power, guys tended to be put off.

"I don't have any harems for you," Cory said. "Just be careful. You were spotted so Nicco—and I have no idea who else—knows you exist. If your buddy Joe finds out you were in public without a guard, he'll freak."

Her buddy Joe...a guy who frequented the bar to beg for her employee discount. He could be quite loyal, but an ogre wasn't much for protection if he was sloppy drunk. "He just comes here because he likes the attention. Every time he gets beat up and tossed from the bar, it's an ego trip. I don't get it, but then I don't understand ogres." She shrugged. "Whatever."

"Between the ogre and the demon, you're marked," Cory said. "You need to be careful."

The concern in Cory's voice got to her. "I know." She'd played with fire and hadn't realized it. "I'll behave."

"Jess, you're not only family, but you're a dear friend. I don't want to see you get hurt." Cory's voice cracked. "Sorry."

"Jesus, Cory." She couldn't lie any longer. "I knew he was a demon. I knew who his minions were from the first. Two chicks. They thought I'd get all starry-eyed over him because he's an actor and when I didn't, it bothered them." Was she attracted to him? Yes. Lane was handsome, but being with him wasn't possible. She wasn't a kid or a giggly school girl crushing on a celebrity. Demons were real. They were the things that went bump in the night. She unfurled her wings long enough to stretch, then tucked them away again. Tending bar with her wings at full extension was cumbersome. "I appreciate your concern. You're one of my few friends, too."

"Just use your head," Cory replied. "Jess, I trust you. You're smart, but you're lonely. I can feel it. You want someone to care about you in a not-so-platonic way. If I could find your mate and hurry things along, I would."

"I know." She appreciated Cory's honesty.

"You're a good faerie and deserve a happy ending," Cory said. "If I could give it to you, I would."

"Yeah. Thanks." She didn't doubt Cory's words. Her cousin did care, but Cory had no idea what Jessica had been through. No one, save for Jinx, Henry and Hestia knew about Jessica's past. They weren't going to tell anyone what she's been through. No way. It wasn't their story to tell.

"Later, tater," Cory said and hung up.

Jessica tucked her phone into her pocket after she silenced the device. She hated taking calls while working and there was no way she'd contact the demon. If she thought about him, she'd consider giving in to him and she'd be in over her head. Nope. No more demons and no more worrying about things she couldn't change. Time to get to work.

* * * *

The next four hours flew by. The barflies

had shown up shortly after she'd opened. Jessica spent the time bustling up and down the counter, slinging drinks and trying to keep some sort of order. Lando, her co-worker, hadn't had a chance to run out for a smoke, either. Even Joe seemed preoccupied.

"Why are we so busy?" Jessica asked. "Is there a full moon?" She dunked margarita glasses in the soapy water. "There has to be."

Mad Dog, a wolf shifter with attitude issues, shrugged. "Everyone heard Nicco's hanging around, but won't come into the bar. Hestia put a protection spell on the joint, so we all think we're safe."

"Until it's closing time." Jessica popped the cap off a bottle of beer. "I've got a bar full of drunk, scared paras. Lovely."

"It's treats," Mad Dog replied. He wandered into the crowd of people milling by the darkened window.

So her mother had protected the bar? Interesting. Maybe she'd allow Jessica to herd the paranormals out through one of the portals.

Rachael, the lone waitress, hurried up to the counter. Her fangs glittered in light. "I need a throbbing pulse and a cool drink." She fanned herself. "He's here."

Jessica reached for the knife she kept behind the bar. "Nicco?"

"No," Rachael said. "Lane Michaels is here. I don't know how he found the bar, but damn. The mage is sexier in person than on television and he makes me hot when I watch his show."

"That's more information than I ever

needed." Jessica snorted. Mage? No. She rolled her eyes. She couldn't be sure, but she had a feeling the photo he'd given her had a tracking spell or something on it for him to find her. Fuck.

"Do I look okay?" Rachael asked. "I want him to like me."

"I'm sure he will because you look fine." Jessica poured a row of shots for the cat shifters at the other end of the bar. "Go talk to him. He'll love you." She wished she'd have seen him first—not because she wanted to be with him, because she wanted to kick him out.

Rachael bounced away, leaving Jessica to the barflies.

"You don't need Michaels," Joe said. "I'll take you home." He tipped his beer bottle to her. "Once you go Joe, you don't go back."

"Honey, I'm not in any position to date anyone, but thanks for the offer—again." She placed a cardboard coaster under his bottle. "Chase one of the cat shifters. They've been eyeballing you."

"Are they?" He wandered down the bar to the gaggle of twenty-somethings, but returned in a moment or two. "Not my speed." He nodded to Jessica. "You know Michaels isn't a mage."

"You can tell?" She filled an order of beers. "How?"

"I can smell him. Mages have the scent of licorice. He smells like burnt paper." Joe finished his beer. "You're sure you don't want to come home with me?"

"I'm working." She wiped down the counter. "What has the scent of burned paper?" She knew damn well, but wanted confirmation. "Fallen angels? Vampires?"

"Demons," Joe said. "Like they'll combust at any time."

"Then he's a demon." She didn't look up at Joe.

"You knew before I did." Joe placed his hand on hers, but didn't grab. "You asked me to test me, but I don't understand why."

"In case I was wrong." She rested her elbows on the counter. "I met him earlier today and I knew what he was. I don't need him in my life."

"You need a good, solid man and I'm offering." Joe swiveled on his stool. "But if the demon keeps you safe from Nicco, then he might not be so bad."

"Who says I want to be with him, first and who says he'll keep me safe? I can hold my own," she said. "I'm not interested in him. How do you know I'm entertaining any thoughts on him?" She'd babbled. Damn it.

"You've unfurled your wings," Joe said. "Cordelia told me one time that a faerie will spread her wings when she's excited. I guess it works for guys, too, but we have other things that salute in addition to wings."

"I could be scared," she said, then tucked her wings away. Damn things. "The demon freaks me out." Liar.

"You don't get scared." Joe narrowed his eyes. "You've kicked more ass than I've ever done."

"I'm afraid of a lot of things," she said. If Nicco showed up, she'd freak the hell out. He'd tried to clip her wings before and would do it again, but this time he'd be successful. She spotted Lane. Her heart skipped a beat and her wings spread again. Fuck. Caroline and Elaine trotted along behind Lane. If he had them and any other way to track her, why had he given her his phone number?

Lane chatted with Rachael and posed for a photo with her before walking away...like he owned the damn place. He strode up to the bar. "Hello darling."

"Hi." Jessica tensed. "Nice tracking spell."

"You wouldn't let me in otherwise." Lane's smile disappeared. "Shit."

"What? Is Hell calling? Do they need you back?" She chuckled. Why wasn't he laughing? Wasn't she funny? When he didn't grin, she sobered. "What?"

"Do you have a portal?" Lane's eyes blazed. His fingernails lengthened into claws. His skin reddened and tongues of fire flickered on his shoulders. "Do you?"

His growl scared her. "Yes. In the basement." What was he feeling that she hadn't?

"Open it." He turned to Joe. "Get everyone to the basement."

"Why?" Jessica held up her hands. "Excuse me, but they've had a lot to drink tonight and I can't comp that much booze."

"Nicco's here." Lane bared his pointed teeth. His fangs gleamed. "Get them out or he'll kill them. He figured out the protection spell and cloaked himself so you can't feel him."

Shit. "Joe, go." She pointed to the back door.

"Now. Nicco's here."

Joe waved his arms. "Everyone, follow me if you don't want to be massacred. Nicco."

At the mention of the demon's name, everyone scrambled. Rachael screamed. She darted from the room, leading the way to the portal. Jessica waved the paranormals out of the bar. "Where is he? How close?"

"I've got this." Lane opened his arms and his body lit with fire. He growled again, this time a thunderous noise that echoed in the now empty bar. "You aren't welcome here."

Jessica ducked behind the counter as a burst of wind shattered the glass in the room. Bottles of booze crashed to the floor. The mirror behind the counter cracked. A scream rang out, but she wasn't sure who'd made the sound. She curled her wings around her body. She might look like a badass who could take on anyone, but not today. She peeked around the bar as the last patrons disappeared down the narrow corridor. When Jessica started toward the door, Caroline landed in a thud in front of her.

"Caroline." Jessica dragged the lifeless woman behind the bar. She needed to help and checked for Caroline's pulse. Nothing. She leaned over her and begged Caroline to breathe. "Come on. You can't die. Don't die. Lane needs you." Demons had a heart, but did it beat? She couldn't remember. Caroline's eyes rolled back and she slumped in Jessica's arms.

"No, no, no," Jessica bit back a cry. She slapped Caroline's face. "Don't you die. Fight it."

Black blood, dead blood, seeped from a

wound along Caroline's hairline. Another pool of blood came from her abdomen.

"Caroline." Jessica willed herself not to cry. She didn't know Caroline, but no one deserved to die like this.

Elaine slid to a stop next to the bar. Her eyes were open and her jaw slack. Black blood dribbled from her lips.

Jessica summoned her courage. She should be fighting off her father and protecting the bar, not hiding behind the counter with dead women.

"Be gone," Lane thundered. A rumble shot through the building. More glass shattered and smoke billowed.

Jessica tugged Elaine out of the fray and placed her beside Caroline. When she knelt next to them, both women turned to dust. Jessica's stomach churned again and she forced herself not to throw up. Demons disintegrated, but seeing the action happen was more shattering than she'd thought.

Lane appeared around the edge of the bar. "He's gone."

She nodded and rubbed her forehead with the back of her hand. "So are they."

He frowned. "Give me your hand. I'm getting you to safety."

She hated being weak. Hated destruction and crying. No matter how hard she tried, she couldn't hold back the tears. "Sure." She allowed him to haul her to her feet. "What's going on?"

Lane crushed her in his embrace and ran through the bar. "Portal?"

"Jesus." She directed him to the bottom

floor of the building and snagged her jacket as they passed her hook. "I shouldn't tell you. Aren't you worried about your minions? They're dust."

"I know." He kept his arm around her and hurried to the portal. "But I'm more worried about you." His words came out harsh, but she detected the note of tenderness.

"You're a demon," she said. "I can't trust you."

"I'm more than just a demon, darling." He grasped her shoulders. "Now, where is the portal? I need to get you to Hestia's house."

"Yeah. Sure." Why was she fighting him? Her father was gone and she had no idea when or if he'd come back. She flicked her fingers and the portal to her mother's house opened.

"Thank you." He pushed her into the portal first, then followed. "Close it."

"You're demanding." She flicked her fingers again. "It's closed." Despite the danger on the other end of the magic tunnel, she relaxed a bit. They'd dealt with one problem, but had a host of new ones waiting.

Lane doubled over and coughed. "Shit."

"What? You tricked me, didn't you?" She wanted to kick him and herself for giving in. "If you told Nicco where I am, I will fuck you up."

"No." He coughed again, then wretched. "Shit. I don't work for Nicco and I fucking hate feeling woozy."

Plenty of individuals barfed at the Sidecar and she'd never felt sorry. If they wanted to drink to excess, then that was on them. She wasn't sure what made him so sick, but she doubted it had anything to do with booze. "What's wrong?" She knelt next to him. "Did I serve you and forget what you've had?"

"No." He wiped his mouth with the back of his hand. "Portal sickness."

"That's a thing?" She'd heard about it, but never saw anyone experience the yuck.

"It is if you're a demon." He offered a weak grin. "We're susceptible to being screwed up in the change of location."

"I didn't know that." She hesitated to touch him. But she had to offer comfort.

"I should've driven you to Hestia's, but I don't know if the car still works or if it's been crushed. It could be destroyed and Nicco would stop us if he knew we were still alive. Besides, I knew the portal would be quicker. Thanks for being understanding. This will pass in a moment."

She rubbed his back. "Take five to gather your wits. What's going on? What does Nicco want this time? He doesn't have to kill paranormals." She knew damn well what her father wanted—her ultimate destruction.

"You." Lane sat in the dirt and gazed up at her. "You know it. He's been biding his time."

She sobered. Lane knew more than he let on. "I do, but how do you know?"

"He says he's collecting, but it's a damn lie. He wants your power. He wants power from each paranormal, but yours is special. It's stronger. If he had his way, he'd get his hands on me, too." Lane sighed. "Your essence is strong."

She leaned against the tunnel wall and stretched her legs. "You're a demon. What can he get from you that he doesn't already have?" She didn't know much about demons—until Lane and her father, she hadn't met any of them.

"I have the key to Hell. I can get you in and out." Lane sighed again. "I'm sorry. The change in pressure gives me motion sickness."

"Here." She conjured a remedy. "*Ornum ipsolum bravada*." She flicked her fingers. "This will help. I'm sorry I didn't try sooner." She offered him the bottle.

Lane drank the concoction and regained his color. He smiled. "Thank you. You're an angel."

"No, I'm not." She hugged her knees. "Remember how you like me when you have to kill me to regain your humanity." She let go of her legs, then stood. "I want to get out of here. I hate basements."

"Jessica." He caught up to her. "I won't kill you. You know that."

"You'll maim me? Remove an arm?" She held onto her jacket. "Whatever. I don't know what you'll do because I don't know you."

"Don't push me away," Lane said. "The last thing I want to do is harm you."

"Why are you bullshitting me?" she asked. "You need my essence, or whatever, to be human again. I'm not interested."

Lane's shoulders sagged. The lines around his eyes deepened and a smudge darkened his right cheek. "I could take your essence, but I don't want to. I have the power and I'm not using it. I don't need to."

"Why? Because you're a gentleman?" She snorted. "I've known many individuals like you.

You're good until it counts, then when your ass is on the line, the only one who matters is you."

"I've been that way, yes." Lane raked his fingers through his hair. "I don't want to kill you and I don't want your essence."

"You don't? I'm not pretty enough? Not what you want? Well, don't tell my mother or my cousins. They'll never let me live it down." She wasn't sure why she'd jumped to defensiveness so fast. Damn.

"Whoa." He curled his fingers under her chin and sparks shot from his hand to her core. "Who says you aren't pretty? You're adorable. You intrigue me. I've never had a woman approach me and not want to know about my sex life, my underwear choices or if I'm single. You're different. You asked about my methods and me. That's huge."

"No one asked it." Giddiness swept through her. She wasn't sure why. She wasn't attracted to him. He was a Goddamn demon. But he did have pretty eyes and a warm smile. She liked his touch and wanted his kiss. Christ, she'd been lonely for too long. She'd bet he tasted good and he'd have soft kisses—at first. The scruff on his cheeks would abrade her skin and send shivers down her spine. She blinked. Shit. So much for not being attracted.

Lane cupped her jaw in both hands. His lips parted.

She tilted her head in anticipation of the kiss.

"No." Lane stayed a whisper away from her. "I can't."

"Can't? Can't what?" If he couldn't kiss her, she'd kiss him. She leaned into him and pressed her lips to his. A moan rumbled in her throat. He was as soft as she'd expected. Her knees weakened and she swiped her tongue across his bottom lip. Where had he been all her life?

Lane broke the connection first. "Stop."

"What?" She blinked. "What's wrong?"

"I'm supposed to deliver you to Hestia. I can't do this. Besides, I haven't brushed my teeth. I can't kiss a lady after...portal sickness."

"Oh." She put space between them. Embarrassment washed over her almost as fully as the time she'd kissed Robby Black because he told her he liked her and he hadn't. He'd lied and thought she'd been too forward. She ended up being the butt of jokes at the bar. "I'm sorry."

He remained close and the muscle in his jaw tightened. "Don't be."

She wriggled away from him and shrugged into her jacket. Determined not to let him see her upset, she walked ahead of him. "I'll get you a toothbrush."

"Jessica." Lane hurried to keep up with her. "It's more than that. It's complicated."

"Sure." She strode up the steps into her mother's house. "We're protected by the spells my mother set, so you're good. I'm here and you're off the hook. Job done. Let me get that toothbrush."

"Jessica." His brow furrowed and the lines deepened again around his eyes. "You don't understand."

"No, I don't, but it doesn't matter. I'm out." She left him in the kitchen and passed Duke in the living room as she made her way to the second floor. Once in her bedroom, she flopped onto the bed and stared at the ceiling. There was nothing wrong with her. No, her problem had to be men. God, men sucked.

CHAPTER THREE

Lane raked his fingers through his hair again. He'd screwed everything up with Jessica. The kiss rocked him to his core, but he didn't trust the reaction. Demonic power could be stronger than his attraction. He wasn't sure if she'd kissed him because she wanted to, or his demon demanded it. What if his human side had won out and she was his soulmate? Jesus. He cared about her. Did she care about him, too?

He strode into Hestia's kitchen. Hestia stopped short and frowned. "What are you doing here?" she asked.

"I delivered Jessica, like you asked." Lane stared at her. "I lost my girls in the blast."

"They knew the risks," Hestia said, her voice low.

"Did they?" He wasn't sure she understood. Hell, he hadn't yet.

"Caroline wanted you to engage Jessica so she could regain her humanity. She didn't care about your feelings and didn't give a rat's ass about my daughter," Hestia said.

He knew that. Caroline was the most self-serving person he'd ever met.

"Elaine wanted to please Caroline, not you." Hestia rested her hands on her hips. The sparkles in her cotton candy pink hair shimmered in the harsh kitchen light. "Why do you look low?"

"I'd like to know when you're throwing me out." He needed to smooth things over with Jessica. Maybe he'd even try for another kiss.

"Throwing?"

"Okay, removing me." He shrugged. "Asking me to go? Huh? You don't like demons and you hate me."

"I didn't say I hated you and since I hired you, I'm not expecting you to go." Hestia narrowed her eyes. "But you're not my favorite person, no."

He fought the urge to roll his eyes. "Then what's the next step?"

"At this very moment, you can't leave," Hestia said. "Nicco knows the house is protected by better, stronger spells than the bar and he's got to realize he'll be harmed if he tries to break in. That said, I can't imagine he hasn't gone looking for weak spots. If you go, then I can't protect you."

"You don't need to. No one here wants me to stay." He stuffed his hands into his jeans pockets. "I'll survive." He'd done so just fine until now.

"It's different."

Ah, but she hadn't said she wanted him to stick around. "I need to get back to film the show." A lie, but he didn't care any longer.

"It's cancelled."

"They're talking about bringing it back for special episodes to finish the storyline."

"You're not a mage."

"So?" Why was he arguing with her? "I could use a toothbrush and toothpaste. The transport gave me motion sickness. Want to help me out?"

"You love to pitch a fit," Hestia said. "You're trying to get tossed."

"Maybe I am." A bit of space between him and Jessica might be what he needed to clear his head. Maybe the lack of proximity would prove he'd jumped the gun on the soulmate thing. Maybe not.

"Enough," she thundered. "You have a job here and I expect you to do it." She flicked her hand and produced both the toothbrush and toothpaste. "Here."

"I—" What job? He'd delivered Jessica. According to Hestia's directive, he was done. He took the items from her. "Where do you want me and is there a bathroom attached?"

"You will go to your room and stay there until required—and yes, there's an attached bathroom," she said. "Understood?"

Before Lane could argue, Duke strode into the room. "Your room is upstairs. Second door on the left."

Lane opened his mouth, but said nothing. He strode out of the room and up the stairway to the second floor. Second door on the left… He tried the handle, then entered the space. At least he had somewhere to crash.

Jessica sat up and her hair fell around her shoulders. "Are you kidding? Go away."

"I can't." He massaged his temples. "Jess, I'm not allowed."

"Oh, yes you are."

"Hestia sent me here." Although she probably wanted him in the next room. Oh well.

"Great." Jessica flopped backwards onto the bed.

"It's punishment," he offered.

"For what?"

"Because my demon made you kiss me," Lane said. His heart ached. He liked her — no demon required. "You kissed me because my demon forced it."

"That's bullshit."

"You don't know that." He knew the truth.

"I don't kiss random men because it's fun." She groaned. "Just go."

"I can't. I'm bound here." Why did it seem like punishment and a reward at the same time? He could be close to Jessica, but not close enough.

"Lovely. I can't kiss you and can't get rid of you. I *am* cursed." She propped herself up on her elbows. "What do we do?"

"I'm not sure." Lane stayed by the doorway. "I've never been in this kind of situation before. If it's any consolation, I can't film my show." It'd been cancelled and the rumors of special episodes were nothing but empty talk, but still.

"Aren't you on hiatus?" she asked. "Like permanently?"

"Yes." He groaned. "May I at least brush

my teeth? I feel gross."

"In there."

She left him alone as he ridded himself of the gross taste. When he headed back into the bedroom, Jessica sighed. "If we're stuck together, then we are. Make yourself comfortable. I need a shower and a change of clothes because I smell like beer and I'm filthy." She left the bed, then disappeared into the adjacent room.

Lane groaned. Having her so close was too tempting. She didn't like him and he cared about her. What rotten fucking luck. He crossed the room and sank onto the bed. Christ. He'd never be able to survive this. Not only did Jessica intrigue him, she hadn't backed down when she'd learned the truth.

Hestia appeared in a cloud of purple sparkles. "Where is my daughter and why are you in this room?"

"Shower." He rested his elbows on his knees. "I haven't peeked and don't plan on it." Well, he'd considered the idea, but wasn't going to act on it with Hestia right there.

"Very good."

"Good? Why is it good? You knew I'd be attracted to her. You're a love faerie. Why would you put us together and not think we'd explore whatever is happening between us?" Lane asked. "Jesus. There is chemistry."

"She deserves better than you," Hestia snapped.

"I wasn't always a bad guy." He'd done rotten things, but he could change.

"You're a demon."

"Faeries can love demons," he challenged. "I was good enough to bring her here."

"You'll want her to regain your humanity." Hestia narrowed her eyes. "You've done your job, but I'm not above cursing you to keep you away from Jessica."

He hated the *'you're a demon'* excuse. "I want to protect her. Nicco will kill her and you know as well as I do, I can keep her safe."

Hestia crooked her eyebrow. "You're not working for Nicco?"

"Didn't you listen to me? He wants to kill me, too, so no. I'm not working for him." He left the bed. "Until today, I might have considered draining a faerie to regain my humanity. I don't want to be consumed by my demon. I can also say it wasn't temptation or being overwhelmed that made me want Jessica. I saw a hundred women with faerie wings stroll around the convention center. One or two were convincing and might have been fun for a night, but they weren't Jessica. The moment I saw her my heart beat again. She didn't give a shit about my celebrity status and saw me."

Hestia glared at him. "You had one job — protect Jessica."

"No, you hired me to get her here and I did that." But he'd gladly protect her from Nicco — hadn't he said that already?

"From him, but also from herself."

"How?"

"She wants to be loved. Cory, Kali…me…we all have someone and she feels left out," Hestia said. "I don't blame her. It's hard to be lonely."

"I hate being lonely, too. I can't imagine she'd want to be on her own." He'd love to fill the void in her life. "Why can't I be there for her?"

"Because she can't have a significant other. She's not a love faerie. She controls life and death." Hestia's eyes blazed. "When I'm gone, she takes over my realm. That's a lot of power that a demon might want to usurp."

"Usurp." He groaned. "No one talks like that, but moreover, that never crossed my mind. I want to be around her because she's funny and snarky. She sees the real me, not the bullshit."

"If you fuck her over, it'll kill her."

"I don't doubt it. No one wants to have their heart broken." What was she getting at?

"You will destroy her because you'll drain her of her essence."

"What if I'm the person who doesn't kill her, but rather makes her stronger?"

"You'll kill her. Demons and faeries don't mix. If you challenge me, I will castrate you." She gave him no chance to argue and poofed from the room.

Lane slapped his hand on the dresser top. Knickknacks toppled over and he righted each of the little faerie statues. His irritation grew. He didn't doubt he could drain Jessica. The darkness tended to overpower everything, but she brought light into his life. He wasn't worried about Hollywood, the show or his other commitments. All he cared about was her. She brought out his protective streak. Christ, he also wanted to kiss her. He wanted her to stick around in his life. He cared about someone besides himself — her.

Jessica padded out of the bathroom. She'd brushed her hair and washed her face clean of makeup. She rolled her eyes. "Hi. I'd though you would've left by now." Her black concert shirt clung to her curvy frame and her blue jeans contoured to her legs. Her wings fluttered as she strode barefoot across the room.

"Hi and no. I'm here for the duration." He'd never seen a more beautiful woman. "Feel better?" He longed to hold and reassure her.

"A little." She finger-combed her hair, working out the curls. "Want to shower?"

"Thank you. I will later." Lane kept space between him and Jessica. His nerve endings were on fire. He smelled her perfume and blood rushed to his cock. Warmth flooded his veins. He longed to keep her in his arms. Her youth and beauty bolstered her strength and he was hooked.

"You're staring." She frowned and folded her arms, stretching the shirt across her breasts.

"You're adorable." No point in hiding the truth.

She rolled her eyes. "Stop."

Was she blushing? Damn, he wanted to make her sigh, scream, blush and whimper again. "I'm telling the truth. If I weren't being threatened with castration, I'd give that kiss another try."

"Castration?" She shook her head. "My mother is so dramatic."

"She cares." So did he.

"I know." She left the room with the towel, then returned empty handed. "I'm tired."

"Me, too." He nodded to the armchair. "I'll

be over here. I know you don't believe me, but I am a gentleman. I won't try to grab you in the middle of the night."

"You saved me from Nicco, so I won't argue." She sighed, then shucked her jeans. "I hated that bar." She crawled between the sheets. "Lando and Joe will need a new place to hang out."

Joe? Lando? A streak of jealousy hit, but he hid his feelings behind a smile. "It wasn't so bad."

"You've been there. It was a dump." She propped herself up on her elbow. "No matter how many spells I used and how much I tried to clean the joint up, the drunks made it a dive."

"I was there once before today," he confessed.

"Ah. Right."

"You weren't there or were hiding in the back." He folded his arms and stretched his legs. "I would've remembered you. No, there was a guy behind the counter."

"Lando. It's only him and me. I begged for more bartenders, but Mother refused."

Her mother owned the bar? No shit.

"Why were you there?"

"Hiding. I wanted to feel normal." He shrugged. "It worked. No one noticed me and I had a beer without being bothered." He nodded to the bathroom. "I'm going to wash up. I promise to keep my hands to myself."

"Thanks." She settled between the sheets and closed her eyes.

Lane forced himself into the bathroom and stood before the mirror. He didn't have a change of clothes. If he showered, he'd have to put his sooty garments back on. He wetted the washcloth and wiped his face. In the morning, he'd ask for the essentials or a chance to go to his penthouse for a change of clothes. The dark circles under his eyes bothered him. He looked tired and rough. Wouldn't his makeup artist have a fit? He'd be hell to make up for the next day's filming. But they weren't filming. Jessica was right. His show was no more. He rinsed out the cloth and draped it on the rack. A good night's sleep would help his appearance and mood. Might get the horniness out, too. He strode into the darkened bedroom.

Jessica had curled beneath the blankets and faced away from him. A dim nightlight burned in one of the electrical outlets. He leaned over her and brushed her hair from her face.

"Night," he murmured. He kissed her cheek. "If you need me, I'm right over here."

"Thanks." She tucked into the pillow tighter.

Although he wanted to crawl between the sheets beside her, he collapsed on the chair. Bone-deep weariness hit and he closed his eyes. Within seconds he fell asleep.

* * * *

"No," Jessica screamed. "Jesus, no."

Lane sat up. He wasn't sure how long he'd been asleep, but the moment she screamed, he became alert. He sat up and spotted Jessica thrashing in bed. She slapped at the air.

"Stop," she screamed again. "Leave me alone. Just stop."

He scrambled to her bed. "Wake up, baby." He jostled her. "It's a dream." He hoped it was anyway. "Look at me. It's only a dream."

"No, stop." She trembled. Jessica threw her arms around his neck and sobbed. "Stop."

He petted her hair and held her. He refused to let anyone hurt her. "I'm here, baby. I've got you."

She continued to sob, but quieter, and pressed her face against his neck.

"I've got you." He rubbed her back. "It'll be okay."

Jessica sucked in a ragged breath and sat back in his embrace. "Lane."

"Right here." He refused to let go. "Are you okay?"

"Yeah." She wiped her face. "I'm sorry."

"No need." He dried her cheeks and rested his forehead against her temple. "What happened?"

"Must've been a dream," she said. "A vivid one."

"You're safe." He tipped her chin, forcing her to look him in the eye. "Are you sure it wasn't a dream? Might have been a spell?"

"Are you trying to get into my head?" She remained close—like the fight was gone from her. "You don't want to see what's in there."

"I'm stronger than you think."

"Nicco tore your body in half." She met his gaze. "He grabbed you by the shoulders and tore you in half like paper."

"I probably deserved it," he said. "I'm not always a good guy." But holding her leveled him.

"In my dream, you were protecting me. I got you killed." Tears streamed down her face and landed on his shirt. "I hate crying, but I hated seeing you die more."

"I won't." He knew better than to kiss her, but acted on impulse. "I'm tougher than you realize."

She brushed her nose along his. "I want the nightmare to end."

"It will." He wasn't sure how, but he'd do his best to keep her safe and happy.

"Stay with me." Her eyes flashed. "Please?"

"I am." She wanted to kill him. The need would drown him, but he'd do whatever she wanted.

"No, right here. I hate being scared." She trembled and curled into him. "Sleep with me."

"I'll do whatever it takes to make you feel protected." He kept his jeans and shirt on and stretched out on top of the covers. "I'm here as long as you want." He tucked her to his side. "You're safe with me."

She cuddled into him. "Thank you." Jessica closed her eyes and went limp. Her wings unfurled and draped across his chest.

Lane sighed. She felt good in his arms. Too good. She smelled like sin and flowers. No, she smelled like home.

Jesus. He'd become attached to her. Good because he had an investment in protecting her, but bad because he couldn't act on his feelings. She had him hard and made him think naughty thoughts. He wanted to kiss every inch of her, hear her scream his name, make her whimper with pleasure, then start all over again.

His cock tented against his zipper. The

pressure added to his pleasure, but God damn it, he needed release.

He closed his eyes. Exhaustion swept over him. Running from fans was easy. Running from Nicco was harder, but keeping his hands off Jessica would be impossible.

His thoughts wandered as he fell asleep. He didn't deserve anyone like Jessica. She might dress in dark clothes, wear heavy makeup and project an air of danger, but she was also a scared woman trying to do her best to keep her fears at bay. She was also innocent and sweet. She glowed. She'd never understand what he'd done and why. She'd want children and a home. The best he could give her was love, but not a future. Who wanted to marry a demon? Especially one who could consume their energy and kill them? No one.

Fuck.

* * * *

Jessica nuzzled the warm male body beside her and sighed. Having a man in her bed was wonderful. She hadn't felt this good in forever. When she opened her eyes, her breath lodged in her throat.

Lane.

Memories from the night before came back in a rush. The nightmares had returned. She'd slept with Lane. Well, not really slept with him—they'd been asleep—not sex…but he was there.

"Good morning." Lane smiled. "Are you okay?"

"I'm okay." She remembered the dream. Every detail came back—standing in the midst of fire, the flames licking her body, Nicco standing over her and cackling as he held Lane by the shoulders. He laughed as he dug his claws into Lane's skin, then tore him into pieces. Her stomach lurched. Fuck. Her dreams hadn't been this vivid before. "I screamed, didn't I?"

"Loud."

"Shit." Her skin flushed. "I'm sorry."

"You had a nightmare. It's expected."

"Still." She met his gaze. "I do that a lot."

"Do what?" Lane asked.

"Dream." She shivered. No matter what she tried—drugs, herbal remedies, meditation, hypnosis—nothing worked.

"We all do."

How could he be so understanding? She shook her head. "You don't get it. I don't dream random things. If I dream about something or someone, the circumstances come true." She didn't want to see him shredded.

"I'm not going to be torn in half."

"It was very real." Her stomach lurched again. "Trust me."

"I do," he said. "You're shaking, baby. It'll be okay. If what you're saying is what's going to happen, we can take steps to change the future now. Right?"

She couldn't get rid of the vision of him in two pieces and very much dead.

"Don't worry. Nicco won't kill me. I'm a demon. I'm already dead." Lane smiled. "I've gone to Hell. Besides, it'll torture me more if he makes me witness whatever he thinks he's going to do to you. He knows there's chemistry between us. He has to know I'm not walking away without a fight."

"Lane." The man was incorrigible and sexy. The more time she spent with him, the more she noticed the little things about him. He might be a demon, but he wasn't evil. He'd helped protect her and fought for her. He hadn't argued with Hestia and instead, he held her. His eyes gleamed when he spoke and his lips were so soft. The scruff on his cheeks caught the light and added to his appeal. She longed to kiss him again.

"What?" Lane clasped her hand in his. "He can't hurt me."

But I can. "Tell me how you became a demon. You weren't born this way."

"Nope." He pressed her hand to his mouth. "Are you sure you want to know?"

"I do." She needed to. Hell, she'd fallen in lust with him and might even consider him a friend.

"I was seventeen. I grew up in Pennsylvania and never thought of my future. Right now was all that mattered. I ran with the wrong crowd and no one cared about me. I doubt my parents know where I am, even now." Lane shrugged. "I wasn't what my parents wanted from a kid."

"You've been on television," she said. "They didn't watch you? Aren't they proud?"

"No idea. I haven't heard from them in years." He stared at her. "They wanted me to be a doctor and straighten out my life. They wanted me to be studious and bring home a nice girl."

"And you settled for me?" she asked. She smoothed the wrinkles in his shirt. "You could've aimed higher than me."

"You're pretty special." He smiled. "If I ever have a son and he brings home a girl like you, I'd be thrilled."

Flatterer. "I guess I'm lucky to have the faeries around. Even the ones that aren't family pretty much are family."

He shrugged again. "I was a bad kid. The faeries and even the gnomes wouldn't have liked me," he said. "I'm guessing my parents were happy to see me go. When I turned eighteen, I was out of there. I said I wanted to see Hollywood and since I'd already been turned...they didn't argue. Anyway, my senior year of high school, I met this girl. Gorgeous girl. Looked like you." He paused and his smile faded. "I fell head over heels for her in a matter of seconds. She invited me to her room and I don't remember where that was, but I went. She might have been from another school—I can't remember. But we did the deed—I wasn't a virgin—and she asked me if I knew the Devil. I was a horny kid. What was I supposed to say? I said, sure I do. When she flicked her fingers, kind of like you do, she summoned a devil."

"A?" She nodded, transfixed. "Shit. Even Hestia can't do that, but it wasn't *the* Devil. Just a minion?"

"Yep," Lane said. "She asked what I wanted and I said I'd like to be a famous actor. I already knew then I wanted to be on television. I'd done time on the high school theater stage and wanted bigger things. I thought it was just pillow talk and a stupid magic trick, but it wasn't. The devil took my soul and I became a demon."

"Are you famous? You seemed to be at the

convention, but that also seems like years ago," she murmured.

"No. Most people didn't watch my show. I'll assume you didn't, either." He grinned. "I'm small potatoes."

"If it's not on the sports channel, I don't watch—but that's only because I'm at the bar most of the time and the patrons don't want to watch anything that's not sporting events."

"Do you like sports?" he asked.

"Football and car racing, but it's because that's all we had on the televisions at the Sidecar," she said. He was the first person to ask her what she liked, rather than assuming she was into sports or drinking.

"Makes sense." He trailed his fingers over the leading edge of her wing. "I'm famous enough. Those who know my show knew me. You saw the line for my autograph and the crowd in that conversation room."

"I did," she said. "You looked miserable." She bit back a whimper. Each time he stroked her wing, he sent sparks straight to her core. She pressed her legs together to stave off some of the tingles.

"I was." He trailed his fingers over her bare arm. "You're observant."

"It wasn't hard to figure out." She stifled the shiver and willed her body not to betray her feelings. Her nipples beaded and heat surged to her pussy. She had to redirect the conversation. "So what you wanted wasn't what you needed?"

"Exactly." He laced his fingers with hers. "I'm not quite what you need, either."

"You'll consume me or anyone else who tries to save you." She hadn't forgotten that tidbit.

"That only happens if he or she isn't my perfect mate." Lane slid his palm over her side, then patted her hip. "I don't actively go looking for souls to devour."

"I bet that makes relationships a bitch." She groaned. Despite the blankets between them, she could feel him and wanted more.

"It does."

"How'd you get Caroline and Elaine?" If she didn't keep him talking about mundane things, she'd jump his bones.

"Caroline wanted to impress me and offered herself up to me," Lane said. "We dated."

"You slept with her and didn't kill her?" Well, shit. Maybe the danger wasn't so bad.

"Not exactly." He blushed. "She blew me and the fires of Hell consumed her. She became my minion while having her lips around my cock. She did so willingly, but she still did it. Elaine wanted out of a bad relationship and had fallen for Caroline. Elaine wasn't a true minion, but she loved Caroline, so she went along with things. She allowed Caroline to take her soul."

"I see." She rested her hand on his. She wasn't just falling in lust. She cared. "Will you kill me?"

"I hope not." He curled his fingers under her chin. "I might be killed, though, if I touch you too much more."

"Why?" She arched into his touch and suppressed a moan.

"If Hestia finds me in bed with you — even

like this—she'll have a fit." Lane brushed his nose along hers. "She warned me multiple times."

"If you were human and showed interest in me, she'd feel the same way." She shoved the bedding out of the way and twined her legs with his. "She thinks I can't handle a man. I have them thrown out of the bar and kicked quite a few cans in my time. I'm not a kid. I've had boyfriends and lovers. I'm not innocent, but you can't tell her that."

"You're every bit a woman," Lane said. He palmed her bare hip. "You're dynamic, but she's right. I can kill you."

"Why?" She'd heard the discussion and remembered what he'd said, but thing didn't make sense. She wasn't happy he'd discussed her with Hestia, either.

"Your energy." He brushed his lips over hers. "Yours is pure."

"No, it's not." She'd lived quite a bit in her thirty-two years. She'd slept around and toyed with magic. She should've been reprimanded years ago, but Hestia didn't.

"You're purer than you realize." He licked his lips. "Faerie magic is potent, too."

"Oh?" Was he warning her? Or coming on to her? She slid her leg along his. "I didn't know that."

"It is." He groaned. "You're trying to mess with me."

"I'm stretching." She unfurled her wings and rubbed her foot over his calf. "Just stretching."

"Jess, you've got me on a hair trigger. I want you." Hunger shimmered in his eyes. "I can't hold back."

She weighed her options. Either die at Nicco's hands or while having a good time with Lane? She'd take the demon every time. "So don't."

CHAPTER FOUR

She'd never craved anyone the way she craved Lane and it both scared and emboldened her.

"Jess." He moved the blankets the rest of the way from her body and slid his hand over her hip until he reached her side and belly. He caressed her, eliciting tingles from deep within her being.

Power and her magic swelled. Her nipples beaded and her pussy clenched. She opened her legs, inviting him to continue touching her. "I need this. Need you."

He turned her on her side and palmed her ass. "Jess." Fire lit in his eyes and he flushed all over. He raked his nails over her skin. When he spoke, his teeth sharpened into fangs.

Jessica marveled at him. Demonic, but human at the same time. If she was going down, then she might as well do it having fun. She shoved her panties down her thighs, then wriggled out of her shirt.

Lane crawled between her thighs. "Christ, you're beautiful." He leaned over her and nipped her inner knee. "I could kill you." He met her gaze. "I'll use up your essence."

"You won't." She wasn't afraid of him. He could destroy her, yet, she wasn't scared. Nicco petrified her, but Lane intrigued her. She shouldn't, but she trusted Lane. "Make love to me."

The hunger in his eyes intensified. "Jess. Are you sure?"

"I am." She threaded her fingers into his hair. Chilly air rushed across her fevered skin and the anticipation of his tongue on her body was almost more than she could take.

"Christ, Jess." He dragged his tongue across her labia. "You smell like sin." He groaned. "And candy." He toyed with her hole. "God, I'm in love."

Fire licked her from within. She groaned. She needed more than to be teased. "Yes."

"Damn, right." He nuzzled her inner thigh. "Like wine." He scraped his teeth along her cunt lips and lapped at her. While he tongued her, he slid one finger into her channel.

She bucked and drew her knees to her chest. Jessica arched her back. "More." It had been too long since she'd been with anyone. Having him touch her, the predatory look in his eyes and the twinge of danger spurred her on. The first sparkles of orgasm started in her belly. "Lane."

"Shit." He sucked on her clit and pumped his fingers. "So good," he said around her skin.

"Uh-huh." She couldn't even breathe—just feel. He'd overwhelmed her. She trembled and squeezed per pussy around his finger. "More."

A rumble vibrated from him to her. Lane nipped her labia, then pulled back and withdrew his fingers. "You're so beautiful." He stood and licked his fingers. "You taste good, too." He unzipped, then shoved his jeans and boxers around his ankles. "So wet. Christ, I need you."

She parted her thighs again. The danger in his eyes and the potential in their coupling excited her. "Take me."

"Damn straight." He stroked his erection. Without words, he lined his cock up with her pussy and pushed. Once fully within her, he whipped his shirt over his head. His tattoos were on full display. His muscles flexed as he moved and his nipples beaded.

She gasped at the fullness of him. He stretched her in a delicious way. She swept her gaze over his naked upper body. A tattoo of the biohazard symbol decorated his ribs on the left side. Calligraphic letters she couldn't read were emblazoned over his heart. An infinity symbol had been inked on his left forearm. Perspiration glittered on his skin.

Lane grasped her hips and built into a steady rhythm. He moved in and out, uniting them in a lover's dance.

She met him thrust for thrust and kept her gaze on his. Lane was magnetic. How had she lived before him?

He leaned over her and held onto her wrists. "Jess."

"Right here," she puffed. "Want you."

"Got me." He pushed into her faster and moved with gusto. He sank balls deep and his eyes flashed. "Shit."

Heat enveloped her. She panted and lost herself in the thrill of being with him. "Lane." The orgasm was close and she trembled.

"Come with me." He let go of her wrists and held onto her hips again. He tipped his head back. His growl echoed in the room.

She shuddered and clamped around him. "Lane." The climax rippled through her. She basked in the wonderful floatiness in her bones. All she saw was him.

"Fuck," he bit out. He slammed into her. His nails bit into her skin. For a split-second, his skin flashed red and his eyes glowed. He curled over her and braced himself on his hands. His hair slipped over his forehead. The glow in his eyes cleared and his skin returned to its natural color.

She draped her arms around his neck. "Is this when I die?"

"No." A lazy smile curled on his lips. He remained inside her. "I'm depleting your power, though. I can't help it. The transference isn't under my control."

"We made love and we're both tired." She toyed with the hairs at the back of his neck. "Maybe that's it. I know I could sleep again."

"Baby."

"Because we had sex." She kept her legs around him. "Crawl between the sheets with me." She needed him there. If she was indeed going to die, then she wanted to go happy. If she wasn't dying, then they could cuddle together.

"Jess." He kissed her. "We'll get caught."

"We will." She wasn't afraid any longer.

"I'll sleep better if you're beside me. I want to feel you."

He hesitated, then pulled out. He left the bed and removed his jeans and boxers. He climbed in beside her. "I didn't take precautions. I'm sorry."

"It's okay." She had to face the truth and tell him. "I can't get pregnant and I'm clean, so there's nothing to worry about."

"Accidents happen." He twined his legs with hers and slid his arm around her waist. "I was careless."

He wasn't upset about her not being able to get pregnant? Maybe he'd missed it. "I'm still here."

"You are," he whispered.

She'd explain why she couldn't give him or anyone else children later. She basked in the post-orgasm glow. "I can't get enough of you."

"Likewise."

"And I'm not complaining." She closed her eyes. "I'm happy."

"Me, too."

She chuckled. "Weren't you more weathered?"

"Huh?" He frowned, forming the lines in his face again. When he smiled, the lines disappeared. He lost the bit of pallor in his skin and his eyes shimmered—like he'd dropped ten years of age in his face.

"You're younger." She trailed her fingers over his cheek. "Your beard is softer and the crinkles around your eyes aren't as deep."

"I hadn't noticed." He kissed her palm. "Your smile is wider and you look happier. Maybe we've made each other better?"

"Works for me." He could use her up or set her free. She didn't care. She was tired, but relaxed. Maybe she wouldn't see the morning, but she'd had one hell of a night so far. She felt cherished. She had Lane in her bed and her life for now — which was more than enough.

* * * *

Lane stretched out beside her. He'd done it—fucked a faerie. But this didn't seem like average sex. They'd made love. How long did she have? He'd felt the power surge. She'd given him her essence, but he'd never been with a faerie before and had no idea how this should go.

Besides, he cared about her. Lane Michaels finally had a heart and wanted to give it to Jessica.

He rolled onto his side and watched her sleep. He'd found a beautiful woman. Dark and moody, yet tender and sweet. He wanted to kiss her everywhere — again.

Jessica curled into him and sighed. Her skin lightened and her hair ran white. Even her lashes paled. An odd smile curled on her lips. He touched her arm and jerked back. Cold. She wasn't supposed to be cold.

"Fuck." He trembled. "Don't you die." Lane hugged her, trying to warm her up. "Jess, don't do this. I'm sorry. I can't lose you. Don't you die."

Jessica began to glow. From head to toe, she emitted white light and grew even colder to his touch.

"No, no, no." He screamed. He'd killed plenty of others in the course of his life, but never anyone he cared about. "Jess, no." A strangled cry erupted from deep within him. "No."

The bedroom door opened and Hestia burst into the room. Her eyes widened and her hair turned pale blue. "I knew I couldn't trust you." She pushed him out of the bed. "Jessica."

He covered his nudity in a blanket and fought the wave of nausea. He'd killed her. He'd started falling for her and before they could explore the relationship, he'd ended her life. "What'd I do wrong?" He knew damn well what, but why not ask?

Hestia glared at him. "You've sent her into suspended animation."

"Huh? Is that how I kill her?" He shook his head. "Everyone else disintegrated."

"No." She stood by the bed and waved her hands. Her wings stretched out and fluttered. She shielded Jessica from his view.

"I want to help," he said. His heart weighed heavy in his chest. "I—this wasn't supposed to happen."

"Did she know what she was doing?" Hestia asked. "Or did you use demon magic?"

"No magic." He clutched the blanket. "She had a nightmare." He wasn't sure what else to say. "She was scared and I reassured her. I had my clothes on and held her. She wanted to take this to the next step." The longer Hestia worked, the tenser he became. This was on him. He'd given in to Jessica's desires—and followed his own, too.

"And you obliged." Hestia turned away from him again and murmured something he couldn't understand. She waved her hands. "A nightmare? What kind?"

"She woke up screaming," he said. "She'd seen Nicco rip me in half."

"You should be." She froze. "She's stable." Hestia whipped around. "Now tell me everything that happened."

Couldn't he get dressed first? Fuck it. "Jessica showered and I chose to sleep on the chair. When she woke up—dressed in her shirt and panties—she screamed. Like blood curdling awful screaming. She was panicked. I didn't know what else to do besides offer her comfort."

"You seduced her."

"It was mutual," he said.

"Right." She folded her arms. The color returned to her hair and dress. "You don't understand what she's been through."

"Then tell me." He needed to know Jessica better. He'd rather hear the story from Jess, but he'd work with what he had. "How'd you stabilize her? Being with me should've killed her. I didn't want to kill her, so I'm thrilled she's at least still breathing."

"You didn't because she's not a full-blooded faerie." Hestia glared at him again. "It's too soon to tell, but you may balance each other out."

He held onto the hope Hestia offered. She might be right. Hadn't Jessica said something about being mates and if that was the case, they'd be the best thing for each other? "Is that why you stabilized her?"

"I put her into a sleep state. Her body is healing from the damage, but you haven't killed her. If she were a full faerie, then she wouldn't need to heal. If she were a full demon like you,

you'd both burn up together," Hestia said.

"Wait." He frowned and sank onto the arm of the chair. "Demon? She's not a full faerie?"

"She's my daughter. I know what she is," Hestia snapped. "You inflicted damage and you don't get that right."

"I'm attracted to Jessica and us being together had nothing to do with my demonic magic. I liked her before I knew she was a faerie. When I saw her at the comic convention, I was drawn to her. I had to find her." He'd poured out his heart. Did Hestia believe him?

"Jesus, then it's true." Hestia sat on the edge of the bed. "She went."

"Stop talking in half-sentences," Lane said. "I'm tired of being left out."

"Jessica isn't a full faerie." Hestia tensed. "Her father was a demon."

"Does she know?" Holy fucking shit.

"I'm not sure," Hestia said. "When the other girls got into princesses and horses, Jessica wanted to learn to fight and insisted on having black balloons at her birthday party. She never liked pink. She's rather have that ratty leather jacket, those awful boots and tattered clothes. She'd rather get dirty than dress up."

"And that makes her a demon? Sounds like she's a tomboy." He sighed. A damn gorgeous tomboy, too.

"It's because that's her personality. I made her a lady as much as I could, but she's broken every mold," Hestia said. "She's the most difficult of my daughters."

"I'm glad she's unique." His desire for her

strengthened. His demon might be attracted to her, but he doubted the demon was in control. Jessica was perfect and the woman he needed to balance him out.

"That doesn't mean she's yours."

"You're talking about her like you can make decisions for her. I'm here to protect her." He'd assumed the job before and fully embraced it now. He'd lay down his life for her.

"You screwed up."

"I found even more reason to do my job to the fullest. I can't love her if she's dead," he replied. "And I *do* love her."

"Love?" Hestia snorted. "Demons don't love."

"I do." He understood, though. "Your demon left. He left an assload of damage and walked out. I bet it pissed you off and cut you to your core."

"Don't get into my head," Hestia snapped. "You can't know how I feel."

"I can empathize." He tucked the blanket in place. "Why is she having nightmares?"

"Ask her."

"I will when she's awake. How long will that be?"

Hestia's glare softened, but the tone wasn't gone from her words. "Soon—unless I'm wrong and you're not her mate. You might have killed her anyway."

He groaned. She wanted to argue. No matter what, she wanted to have this out. "You're not dead." He stared at her. "If faeries and demons can't mix, then how are you still here?"

"I'm the strongest faerie."

"What if Jess has the same resiliency? What if she's got the healing power of the demon and the heart of the faerie? She has your strength and courage." Lane bunched his free hand. "It's possible." She was the best of both worlds and everything he wanted in a woman.

Hestia narrowed her eyes. "When I look at Jessica, I see her father and it kills me. She's the spitting image of him. My heart breaks all over again because I know he didn't care. I was a notch on his belt and she means nothing to him."

"She meant something to him," he said. "He needs her."

"Maybe." Hestia paused. "I'm not convinced Jessica is the one perfect embodiment of love for you. I'm not sure you're worthy of her. Don't punish her because you're not going to be the man she needs."

He stared at the older faerie and gritted his teeth. He'd love to be dressed for this argument, but the more he talked to her, the more she angered him. He wasn't good enough for Jessica. Was any man? But moreover, was Hestia punishing Jessica for something she couldn't control? She didn't have the power to decide who her parents would be or who fate decided she'd love. "Don't knock Jessica because of a decision you made. She's more than you give her credit for being."

Jessica gasped and sat up. "Holy shit." She shoved her hair out of her eyes and glanced about. "Where am I and why am I naked?" She met Lane's gaze. "We..." Her gaze shifted to her mother. "Shit."

Lane sat beside her on the bed. "We're naked together," he muttered." He covered her nudity with the sheet. "How do you feel?"

The muscle in Jessica's jaw tightened. "Honestly? I feel great."

"The spell." Hestia nodded. "I brought you back."

"Ma, you didn't. I wasn't dying." Jessica smiled. "Not at all."

Not dying? Lane tensed. Then what had happened?

"Jessica, the demon...you know what you did with him." Hestia shook her head. "You knew better."

"Yeah, we horizontally tangoed." Jessica shrugged. "I enjoyed it."

Lane's ego inflated. He'd make the next time he and Jessica were together even better. He'd take his time and worship her.

"Jessica," Hestia bit out. "Enough."

"I'm not a kid," Jessica replied. "I'm over thirty."

She didn't look a day over twenty-five. Lane eased his arm around her, giving her comfort.

"He's a demon," Hestia said. "A spawn of Hell."

That was low...but true. Lane sighed. "So?"

"He's not Dad," Jessica said. "If he were, he wouldn't be here right now."

Lane toyed with the wrinkles in the sheet. She had a point. If Jessica wanted him around, he'd stay. He'd do whatever she wanted. Christ. For being a scary demon, she had him wrapped around her finger.

"Dad was a jerk. Still is. That's why he wants to kill me," Jessica said. "I'm a threat. Now that I've survived demon sex...I'm even more dangerous to him."

"Don't say that." Hestia crinkled her nose and her hair turned pink. "It's not lady-like."

"I'm no lady." Jessica folded her arms. "Never have been."

"Wait." He tipped Jessica's gaze. "You're going to explain this all to me, right?"

"I wish you hadn't figured this out, Jessica." Hestia shook her head. "You weren't supposed to know."

Jessica held Lane's hand. "Until a very short time ago, I'd never met my father. Ma swore he'd died and I believed her, but I knew better. The reason Nicco wants to kill paras and me in particular, is because he's a paranormal, too. He's a demon."

"*The* demon." Lane sagged against the headboard. "Fuck." No wonder Hestia was so touchy and Jessica hesitant to be with him. "I'm not like him."

"I know." Jessica leaned into him. "But you *are* a demon. You can't go against Nicco."

"Your father," he said. The words and the weight of the situation sank in. "Shit."

"Exactly." Jessica nodded. "Now do you still want to be with me?"

"I knew he'd change his mind." Hestia shook her head again. "Get dressed. You've been relieved of your service, Mr. Michaels."

"The hell I have been. Who says I can't go against a bully? I didn't chase Jessica only to quit when things get hard." He turned to Jessica. "I refuse to let that jackass, even if he is your father, hurt you because he's got a vendetta. You're mine. You're my kryptonite...my girl. I'll move Hell to keep you safe."

"I'm a faerie." A slight smile curled on Jessica's lips. "Not a lady."

"You're a demon faerie, which is pretty bad ass." Lane rubbed her bare shoulder. "I'm in awe."

"Are you?" Jessica crinkled her nose. "We set rules. Remember? No nookie-nookie. Guess we screwed that up."

"Rules are meant to be broken." He rested his forehead against hers.

"We'd better quit the sex talk while my mother is still in the room." Jessica grinned. "Respect and stuff."

"Of course." He put space between them and turned to her mother. "I'm sorry."

"You'll mess her up in the same way Nicco messed with me." Hestia pointed at Lane. "My earlier threat still remains. I will castrate you, demon, if you hurt her." She turned on her heel and left.

"That went well." Jessica rested on her side and stretched out beneath the sheet. "Just don't tell me you love me. Love doesn't exist. It's bullshit."

No it wasn't and he'd prove her wrong. "What are the other rules, since we're alone now?"

"We're only a couple because you're protecting me. Nothing else," Jessica said. "I won't use you and you don't use me."

Lane leaned in close and whispered in her ear. "You will explain why you glowed and we will make love again. No fucking. We'll make love."

She shivered, then narrowed her eyes. Her lips parted, but no sound came out.

"I fully expect you to be on your guard." Lane stretched out with her. "But I do have your back." And front and everywhere else.

"I know." Jessica left the bed and strolled, fully nude, across the room. He noticed the tattoo of faerie wings on her ribs when she faced him. "Nicco wanted my mother's power. I don't know what the exchange looked like, but I believe I glowed because of you. We are a power source for each other. You're stronger now. Any injuries you might have had are healed. You're wide awake...hungry. Horny."

"I am." She wasn't wrong. "So?" Did that mean they could make love again? If she didn't cover up, he'd take her against the wall.

"I'm fully charged."

"Good." Then she was ready for round two.

"Nicco told my mother he'd be back. He said he only loved her. I don't know if she glowed or if he gained power, but I know why he wants paranormals. He's trying to find me."

"He knows where you are," Lane said. "He found you at the bar, but I stopped him."

"Right, but killing a few paras along the way helps add to his power in smaller increments." Jessica leaned against the bathroom door frame. "He's evil."

"He wants to purge you of your power." Lane left the bed and joined her by the bathroom. "What if you find your mate? Won't that stop him?"

"You're not my mate."

The hell I'm not. "How do you know?"

"Because you're a demon? Ma and Nicco were a bust. We would be, too," Jessica said.

"Let me prove otherwise to you." He needed to. "I can't walk away and it has nothing to do with protection."

"Lane."

"I didn't kill you when we made love," Lane said. "I had no idea about the power exchange and now that I know, it doesn't change my feelings. If I were truly bad for you, you'd be dead. You're not. If we didn't have something special, your mother wouldn't be having such a fit."

"You've lost your mind."

"Nah." He held her hands. "We energized each other. We're meant to be in this together—whatever *this* is."

"You're not serious." Jessica reached for him, then pulled back.

"I am. We've changed, yes. Your wings are darker and hair is deeper black. You've grown stronger." He gathered her in his arms. "You powered me up, yes. We're strong apart, but I'm convinced we were meant to find each other. You don't make a habit of going to the comic conventions, do you? I don't make it a habit to chase women who show up for autographs."

"I lived because my mother stepped in," Jessica said. Her tone flattened. "Right?" She shrugged away from him.

"You know better than that." He grasped her wrist. "Don't do this. Don't put space between us. If you're scared of what will happen, then tell me. The more you hide, the more I'll push. Your old man is a dick. He's not worthy of you. I'm not him and I try not to be a dick. I'll treat you like a queen." He tugged her close again. "When we made love, I felt human again. Not soul-saving human, but real. Like I've never felt before. I want that feeling back because I want you."

She hesitated. "I'm not sure how to feel."

"Give us a chance. You deserve more." Lane held her and delighted in the feel of her body against his. "I'll bet you're stronger than you realize and more than Nicco expects."

"Me?"

He nodded. "You."

Jessica sagged into him. "You're going to be the death of me."

"Never." His heart belonged to her and he'd offer his life to save her. She'd be the death of him and he wouldn't argue.

CHAPTER FIVE

Jessica rested her head on his shoulder. She needed normalcy. Then again, she needed space between her and Lane. She craved him. That had to be dangerous. Right? Her life was in turmoil; her father wanted her dead. Was it wrong to want life to go back to how it had been before the threat?

"I need to wash my clothes. Want me to throw your stuff in the load?" she asked. "I'm heading that way."

Lane curled his fingers under her chin. "You can, but you don't have to."

"When we haven't been naked, you've worn the same clothes for two days. Washing your clothes is the least I can do." Plus, doing the laundry would give her time to think. "You could grab a shower."

"Okay." He let go of her and picked up the pile of his clothes. "Thank you."

"No problem." She ogled his ass as he headed into the bathroom. God, he had a spankable butt. She'd grabbed his rump during sex and loved it. The longer she stared at his ass, the more she frowned. "Do you really have a pentagram on your ass?"

He stood in the bathroom doorway with a towel low on his hips. "What, babe?"

Babe? Her frowned deepened. At this rate, she'd have to use product on her face to get rid of the lines. "You have a pentagram on your ass."

"I'm a demon. We all have one like that." He shrugged. "You probably have something similar on yours."

"I do not." She folded her arms. "Will it go away if you regain your humanity?" She needed to find a mirror so she could check out her own backside in search of a mark she'd never seen before.

"I don't know."

"Oh." She heaped her clothes into the basket and added his to the pile. "Just wondered."

"Do you want it gone?"

"It's not my ass or my decision." She headed across the bedroom and selected an outfit for the day, then dressed. Her brassiere bit into her skin and her panties chafed. She donned one of her favorite concert T-shirts and soft jeans, then padded barefoot into the hallway.

"Babe?" Hair wet and skin glistening, Lane ducked his head into the corridor.

"Lane?" She paused. Why was he calling her his babe? Hadn't he understood the rules?

"Just needed one more look." He grinned, then winked. "Don't be long."

"I won't." An odd tingle shot down her

spine. She descended the stairs to the ground floor. Once in the laundry room, she tucked the clothes into the washing machine. She expected to hear her mother or Duke moving about the house. Her mother loved to sing—badly—while doing housework. Duke tended to follow Hestia wherever she went in case she needed him. She paused before she hit the start button on the machine. The silence unnerved her. Was there a note? She abandoned the washing machine and ventured toward the kitchen. She crept across the house and almost called her mother's name, but hesitated. A scratching noise caught her attention. What the hell?

She tiptoed into the main corridor, then to the doorway leading to the living room. A smell curled around her and churned her stomach. She'd only ever noticed that particular aroma once before...when Jinx had died. Something red stretched across the floor.

"Ma?" she whispered and followed the red stain. When she rounded the hutch, she stopped in her tracks. Duke—or what was left of him—had been left in a crumpled mess on the carpet. Blood gushed from his chest and a wound on his neck. Hestia wasn't visible. Jessica fought the scream in her throat and the wave of nausea threatening to overwhelm her. How long had Duke been there? She and Lane had been holed up in her bedroom for the last few hours. She'd given her mother and Duke little thought.

She turned on her heel and sprinted from the scene. Jessica collided with a strong body on the steps. "Stop." She pounded her fists into the man's chest. "Stop." When she pushed, he held tight.

"Jess." Lane, in another towel, hauled her into the first room. "What's wrong?"

"He's dead." Panic rose within her and her wings fluttered. "Duke's dead."

"I know." Lane held her to his chest. "I'm sorry."

"How do you know?" She balled her hands and pounded against his chest. "What did you do?"

"I didn't do anything." He placed his finger over her mouth. "I feel Nicco in the house. That's who killed Duke."

She shuddered and her panic increased.

"I don't know why he did it. Duke wasn't hurting him." Lane's eyes lit with fire. "But a demon knows when other demons are around, so Nicco senses me, too."

"Shit," she blurted.

"It's not going to be a picnic, no." Lane's lips curled in a sneer. His sharp teeth glinted in the low light.

She tensed. "Lane, don't do it. Don't give in to him."

"I'm not." He shook his head. "No way."

"How do I know you won't change your mind?"

"Hush."

She wanted to argue, but didn't. She'd heard the click...of a gun? Knife? Door opening? She wasn't sure. "He's here."

Lane nodded. "Do you have a portal?"

"Downstairs," she said. She shivered. "But the window in my room could work for escape. I can try to fly us out of here." She wasn't sure her wings were strong enough to fly them both, but she had little choice. "Hold onto me."

"Jess?" He dipped his head once. "I'm with you. What do we do?"

"Hold on. I'll fly us out of here." She threaded her arms around him.

"Wait. We'll go to my place." Lane shook. Thick black wings unfurled from his back. He stretched and the wings blotted out the moon. "I've got you." The landscape blurred and chilly air caressed her skin.

Her stomach lurched. Normally, she had no issues with flying. But going faster and higher than normal, weakened her reserves. She held onto him and buried her face against his neck.

Within seconds, she and Lane were far from Eriewood. She didn't recognize her surroundings. She closed her eyes. She couldn't get the vision of Duke's mutilated body from her mind.

Lane slowed and placed her on her feet. She had no idea where he'd taken her, but if she was far away from Nicco...good. "Where are we?"

"My penthouse." Lane tucked his wings away. "I live here while we film the show." He stepped into the apartment. "I don't have spells to keep you safe, but I know when he's coming. We've got a good head start."

"He doesn't know where you live?" She rubbed her arms. "I don't like this."

"I'm sorry, babe." He tugged a pair of jeans from the dresser and donned the garment before he gathered her in his embrace. "Nicco doesn't know where we are and my neighbor is a shifter. He'd also know if Nicco showed up."

She nodded and tucked into him.

"Why does he want to kill you? Because you're too strong for him?"

"I can kill him." She trembled. "Faeries can be drained by demons, yes, but I've got the powers of the faeries and the demons. I can heal myself and could heal you—just not Duke because he was already dead."

"And Nicco wants to either kill you or own you so he'll never die."

"Yes." She turned away from Lane, but kept him in her peripheral vision. Tears burned at the corners of her eyes. "He doesn't know that I know."

"He will." Lane kept space between him and her. He donned a black T-shirt. "Come here." He didn't give her the chance to respond before he embraced her again. He petted her hair. "We need to work together."

"Don't say because I can heal you," she murmured. She couldn't handle being used by another man.

"Because I can feel him coming and you have the power to destroy him. Together, we can break him," Lane said. "You've got the upper hand because you can break his heart."

"How?" She wasn't following Lane's logic at all.

"Because of me."

"I don't understand."

"You didn't kill me and I didn't destroy you. Jess, we're meant to be together."

He'd tried too hard to convince her, but he

made sense. "We can't be fated to be together." Who was she kidding? They should both be dead and the only logical answer was fate wanted them together.

"We can." He kissed her. "I feel alive because I'm with you, not because of your power. You make me want to be a better man."

She shook her head, despite agreeing things were better when he was around.

"You don't believe me, but it's true."

Jessica sighed. A dull ache formed behind her eyes. She hadn't been able to process her surroundings, let alone her true feelings for Lane and now she had no choice. She had to work with him to survive. "Do you know why I can't have children? Faerie babies?"

"No."

"My mother had me—her words—fixed. She said I wouldn't be a good candidate for motherhood." She shook her head and scrubbed her hand across her forehead. "Isn't that silly?"

"No. It's fucked up." He curled his fingers under her chin. "But whether you can have children or not doesn't matter to me. I like you the way you are. Besides, I don't know if I could share you."

She snorted. "Thanks." He knew how to make her feel better. "I was afraid to tell you."

"Don't be." He kissed her. "I'm not that scary. I won't get rid of you. You might have to get rid of me…"

"That could be arranged." She blew out a ragged breath. Things weren't so bad. A voice whispered in her mind. *He destroyed Duke. I fought back and have been banished to Hades. I can't help you.*

Jessica massaged her temples. She knew the voice—her mother. "Hades?" She sagged to the floor. The pain in her head increased. "Ma?" Her stomach churned and she refused to believe what she'd been told. Her mother couldn't be in Hell. How was she supposed to destroy Nicco without the teensiest bit of help from her mother? A gut-wrenching sob overwhelmed her. She hated to cry, but couldn't stop.

Lane gathered her in his arms again. "Babe." He petted her hair. "I've got you. Tell me what happened. What's wrong?"

She couldn't catch her breath. Her body ached. She curled into Lane. "Nicco…killed Duke."

"I know," he soothed. "I'm sorry, babe."

Her voice caught. "He banished my mother to Hades."

He swayed with her. "Demons do that."

She wiped the tears from her face. "Why? What did she do that deserved banishment to Hades?"

"Because we're assholes." Lane kissed away her tears. "Well, some are. If he banished Hestia to Hades, then he had a reason. We're supposed to live in Hades. He could be kidnapping her to win her back or to keep her from someone—probably from you."

"That's fucked up," she murmured.

"Never said it wasn't." He kept her in his arms and walked over to an oversized armchair. He settled on the cushion and pulled her onto his lap. "It could be he's punishing someone. Might be her for leaving him. Might be her for moving on after they split. Or...he could be punishing you."

"Why?" She hadn't done anything. "He's my father. So what if I have as much power as he does? That doesn't mean I want to use it. I don't like conflict."

"I don't know why, babe." He rested his forehead against hers. "He could be doing this just to be an asshole."

She allowed herself to cry the rest of her tears, then summoned her courage. She refused to let Nicco—father or not—do this. He'd killed enough and deserved punishment. "Will you help me eliminate my father?"

"Whatever you want to do, I'm in." Lane wrapped his arms around her and kissed the tip of her nose. "What do you want to do?"

"Destroy him," Jessica said. "If he's my father, then I'm part demon. Right?"

"I believe so." Lane nodded. "You have faerie and demon blood, yes."

"And a demon on my side?" She needed to hear the words one more time.

"Yes."

She draped her arms around his neck. "Thank you."

"I knew from the moment I first saw you that I'd be in your life," Lane said. "I didn't think of saving myself. I thought I'd found my other half."

His words sent shivers down her spine and encouraged her belief they could do this. They could survive and come out on the other side together. But, she knew the truth—they could both die for their troubles. "Remember that when we're both frying in Hell because I couldn't win against my father."

"My faith's in you." He slid his hands down her ribs to her waist, then hips. "You've got the determination and desire to make this work. I have no doubt you'll kick some serious ass."

Her heart hammered. She'd never had anyone in her corner before. Her father hadn't wanted her, mother hadn't been proud of her and her sisters weren't around any longer. All she had was him and her own resolve to survive. She could do this — she could win.

* * * *

Lane scooped her into his embrace and carried her across the room. He didn't have much time to romance her, but damn it, he wanted this to be memorable. He placed her on the bed. "Sexy faerie."

Jessica removed her shirt, turned her back on him and extended her wings. She glanced over her shoulder. "What are you going to do?"

"This." He eased up behind her and trailed his fingers along the leading edge of her wing. He kissed her bare shoulder. He needed to touch her everywhere. She smelled like heaven. Each whimper and mewl turned him on. Blood rushed to his groin and heat filled his being.

"Lane." She leaned into him.

He nipped at her neck, then down to her shoulder. He slid his arm around her midsection to cup her breast.

Another mewl escaped her throat. "Lane, yes." She unhooked her bra, exposing her breasts. "More."

"Yes." He massaged her breast, rolling her

nipple between his fingers. He appreciated her curves and the way she reacted to him. Every time she bucked against him, she spurred him on. He slid his free hand between her legs.

Jessica parted her thighs. "I want to be adored."

"You are." He opened her jeans and worked his hand beneath her panties to caress her pussy lips. So wet. Christ. He needed to taste her. He scraped his fingernail across her clit and sucked on her neck at the same time.

Jessica rested her head on his shoulder. She placed her hand over his on her breast. "Need you."

"I'm here." He breathed her in. "Always."

She groaned. "I want more."

He loved how she overwhelmed him. She tugged his hand away from her chest and worked his other hand out of her jeans. Without a backward glance, she left the bed long enough to remove her clothes, then crawled naked on her hands and knees across the bed. She rested on her belly in front of him and made quick work of opening his pants. "No briefs?"

"Not all the time." He threaded his fingers into her hair, guiding her. "Not with a hot woman in my arms. I want to be ready."

"I'm in your bed and naked." She traced the seam of her mouth with the blunt head of his erection. Before he could speak, she sucked him to the back of her throat. She bobbed her head.

"Oh Christ." He held onto her hair, but she set the pace. Each time she tugged him in, she flattened her tongue along the underside of his cock. At the same time, she fondled his balls. A shiver ran through his being. His demon was on high alert because she brought out his human protective streak. The demon wanted to keep her. His balls grew heavy and the first tingles of orgasm started in his belly.

Jessica hummed and the vibration pushed him right to the edge. He pulled out. If he didn't stop, he'd never be able to. "Shit."

"Yes?" She licked her lips and batted her lashes. "What's wrong? Didn't you like what I did?"

Her mix of innocence and sexiness added to her appeal. "You'll make me come without being inside you."

"So?" She offered a naughty grin.

"Turn around." He whipped his shirt off and stepped out of his jeans. He stroked himself. One or two more tugs and he'd come. Fuck.

Jessica propped herself up on her hands and knees once more. She wriggled her ass. "Better?"

"Damn." He grasped her hips. With one thrust, he buried himself to the hilt within her. He groaned and moved on instinct. The sound of skin on skin echoed in the room. He pushed deep, then pulled most of the way out. Another moan rumbled in him and he teetered on the edge of orgasm. His demon roared, wanting to change her. He held back—she didn't deserve to be a minion. He'd rather have a partner.

"Lane." She met him thrust for thrust and writhed.

He reached around her waist and tweaked

her clit. "Ready?"

"Like yesterday."

He moved within her, like they were one body. She owned his heart. He never wanted someone in the same way he craved her. His restraint snapped. "Fuck. Come with me."

"Yes." She moaned. Her movements turned jerky and her wings fluttered. She tilted her head back, then curled forward. "Oh my God."

She'd said the words on his mind and stolen his breath. He embraced the orgasm and moved with abandon. She overwhelmed him. He surged into her and shuddered. "Fuck." He added a few more thrusts then slumped over her.

Jessica settled on the bed. "You wore me out." She grasped his fingers. "I loved it. Do you know you focused me?"

"I did?" He kissed her shoulder. "Good."

"I can face anything."

"Because we had sex?" he asked. He wasn't following her.

"Because you made love to me." She glowed, but unlike the first time they'd had sex, she continued talking to him. "I'm stronger."

He felt stronger, too. Was he? "I'm glad."

She sighed. "Thank you."

"Making love with you isn't a hardship." Now he knew he wasn't going to kill her, he wanted to fuck all over again.

Jessica tensed. "Shit."

"What?" He tried to surface from the fuzz surrounding his thoughts. "What do you feel?"

"Get dressed. Nicco's close." She nudged him. "Now."

He scrambled off her. Their clothes lay in a crumpled mess on the floor. "I've got a shirt and a pair of jeans you'd fit into."

"I've got this." She stood and snapped her fingers, conjuring a full outfit for them both. "Done, but I want to wear your jacket."

He glanced down at the jeans, fresh shirt and boots she'd clothed him in. Her threadbare T-shirt cupped her ample bosom and her jeans clung to her frame.

"Of course." He met her gaze. "Do you know what you're going to do?"

"I've got a pretty good idea."

CHAPTER SIX

Lane draped his leather jacket around her shoulders. He could make love to her a thousand times and not have enough. Right now, they had to focus. "How do you want to do this?" If she had a plan, he'd follow.

Jessica snuggled into his jacket. "I'm not up on my demonic lessons. Where's the demon's weak spot?"

"It all depends on the demon. If you want to take down a demon, you need strong magic and grit." He folded his arms. He'd rather be loving her and exploring her body all over again, than fighting anyone. He hated brawling, but she needed help. "You can't let up. He'll use everything against you and won't stop. He'll bring up things you don't want to deal with and use the full power of his demon. He'll insult, strike and anything else he can come up with. He'll bring up your mother, your past, your family, you not being enough…the choices you've made that others see as poor." He'd tried to think of everything and every time she winced, he wished he could take the words back.

"He'll use hand-to-hand combat, too? Won't he?"

"Demons prefer head games and verbal barbs," Lane said. "We like to fight where we think we have the high ground. Physical combat isn't it, but we will resort to it. He'll torture you before he'll kill you. It's more fun to be in your head and get you to second guess everything than death. Death is too easy."

"He wants to play with me, even if it's fucked up." She rolled her eyes.

"Yes." He stared at her. She was stronger than she realized. She understood Nicco, better, too. Instead of barging in to make her stand, she wanted intel.

"Stand back." She wriggled her shoulders, shrugging out of the jacket and opening her wings "I really want to wear this longer, but my wings won't be contained."

"I'll hold onto it for you." He loved the way she'd filled out the garment. The thing looked better on her than him anyway.

Jessica bound her hair into a ponytail. Determination shimmered in her eyes. "He's on our trail. I feel it."

He tipped his head. He sensed the change in the wind. "I'm following your lead. He's close."

She grabbed the front of his shirt. "Be completely honest with me right now. Do you love me?"

"Yes," he said, with no hesitation.

"Would you die for me?"

"Yes — I hope that doesn't happen, but I will." He tucked his fingers in her front pockets. "You're very important to me. Next?"

"Can he manipulate you in order to screw with me?" she asked.

"He can't make me say what I don't feel, but he can silence me and tell you what his interpretation of what he thinks I feel." He paused. "He'll shut me up and say I've turned on you. That's not true. I love you so much. If you killed me, I'd die happy because I had you in my life."

"Charmer."

He shrugged. Why lie? "You asked for honesty."

"I did." She stood nose-to-nose with him, her mouth a whisper away. "He can kill my mother's boy toy and banish them both to Hades, but he can't have me."

"Good girl." He kissed her. "You've got this."

"I hope so." She kissed him back and rested her forehead against his. "Let's go."

Lane almost asked her where they were going, but didn't. If she was going to fight, she had to lead. Demons sensed weakness. If she had any second thoughts, Nicco would pounce.

Jessica strode up to the roof of the building. The wind whipped her ponytail and her cheeks were stained crimson. "Where are you?"

Lane stood beside her. He'd use every last ounce of his magic to protect her.

Light flashed before them and Nicco appeared. He sneered, then shrugged. "I knew you'd call for me." He stuck his hand out and pinned Lane to the wall.

Lane thrashed, unable to remove himself from the bricks.

"Right, because you know everything." Jessica said. "Blah, blah."

Saucy, but she'd gotten under the demon's skin. Lane nodded.

"What a mouth. Does your mother know you talk that way?" Nicco asked. He stalked toward her.

"Demon's don't parent." Jessica checked her fingernails, then rubbed them on her thigh. "Probably just as well."

Lane bit back a grin. She'd hit right on target. He wished he could communicate through their thoughts. If he could, he'd encourage her to keep going.

"Enough," Nicco shouted. "No one talks to me in such a manner."

"Who do you think taught me to stick up for myself?" Jessica cocked her hip. "Momma parented where you failed. She was my mother and father."

"Do not challenge me," Nicco thundered.

She'd hit another bull's eye. Lane's heart beat faster with pride. What did she need him for?

"I'm not a child," Jessica said. "And I'm not afraid of you."

"No?" Nicco snarled. "You look scared. Your mother was, too."

The asshole. Lane wished he could give Jessica his strength.

"You put my mother in Hades. That's not a

picnic." Jessica notched her chin in the air. "What else do you have? My demon? Yeah, I know. He'll kill me. It's old news." She shrugged.

Good girl, even if she liked to live on the edge and push the demon.

"I'm good with Ma being on vacation. I needed some separation from her. She's been too clingy." Jessica taped her foot. "What else have you got?"

"You can't outgun me." Nicco glared at her. "The demon told you what to expect. He's wrong. He wants his humanity and he'll say anything to regain it. You're no better. You've been duped."

Goddamn it. How dare he plant doubt in her head? Lane thrashed against the spell binding him to the wall.

"I know what he wants." She shrugged again and admired her fingernails. "He thinks he'll get his humanity, but he won't. I took his power. Aren't you proud of me, *Daddy*? I'm underhanded and despicable just like you."

Lane bit back the shred of disgust. He trusted her, but the words still hurt. He hated being out of commission. But if he were beside her, Nicco wouldn't believe her.

"Your actor isn't worthy of you," Nicco said. "He'll steal your power, too. Come with me and you'll be strong without him. A good woman doesn't need a man."

"Daddy, for the first time in my life you're right. I don't need him." Jessica straightened her shoulders. "But the show can't recast him, so I can't kill him. I'm having too much fun playing with him. He's like catnip."

Lane relaxed. He'd be her catnip all day long.

"His minions need him, too." Jessica strode up to her father. "But...they're all expendable. I'm growing tired of them."

"Good girl. Everyone is expendable." Nicco glared at Lane. "You trusted the wrong faerie, demon."

Jessica threw her arms around Nicco's. "I've been afraid of you for too long. You're the being I need in my life." She unfurled her wings in a rush. The snap echoed. "My father."

"Of course. You're not strong enough without me." Nicco bared his fangs. His skin reddened and fire burned in his eyes. "Foolish girl. You thought you were worthy of me."

"Jessica." Lane's voice cracked. He wanted to snatch her from Nicco's grasp.

"Foolish?" Jessica pulled a butterfly knife from the air. "Never underestimate a pissed-off faerie." She plunged the blade into Nicco's neck. "You lied to me. You killed my mother's boyfriend. You killed my friends." She twisted the knife, then pulled it out only to plunge it in again. "You ruined my bar and wrecked my source of income." Her wings extended and darkened. "You don't want me." She withdrew the knife, then stabbed a third time. Blood spurted everywhere and gushed from the wounds.

"Never did want you," Nicco roared. He dug his claws into her arms. His horns extended and his muscles bulged. "You can't kill me."

"Bullshit." She yanked the knife forward, slashing it across Nicco's throat. Black, dead blood poured from the gaping wound.

Lane slid down the wall. "Keep doing it," he screamed. "The weaker he gets, the more his deeds are undone."

Jessica twisted the knife again. "This is for Ma, for Duke, for my friends and for Lane…and for me."

Nicco's eyes rolled back in his head. His skin paled and the fires dampened. He sagged to the ground.

Jessica shoved the carcass out of the way. The wind whipped her hair and soot darkened her cheeks. Her wings fluttered. Lane paused. Christ, she was beautiful.

Lane sprinted up to her. "Are you okay?" He grasped her biceps. Tears streamed down her cheeks. "Babe," he murmured and tucked her to his chest. "You did what had to be done and are a hero."

She clung to him. "I killed him."

"I know." He petted her hair. "You'd never be free of him otherwise. Now you can live your life without having to deal with that hanging over your head."

"What about you?" She leaned back in his embrace and blinked the tears from her eyes. "I'm part of him. Will I have the desire to kill you, too?"

"Not unless you go rogue." He rested his forehead against hers. "And I don't think you ever will."

Her youth, as well as the weight of the world, showed on her face. Still, she struck him as beautiful—his beautiful warrior. She wiped her cheek. "You said I reversed the magic. Does that mean Caroline and Elaine will come back?"

"No." He shook his head. "That's not reversable."

"Oh." She threaded her arms around his neck. "I'm sorry."

"It happens," he said. "You hit below the belt with the line about my humanity. You wounded me." He met her gaze and bumped noses with her.

"It's not true." She toyed with the hairs at the base of his neck. "You've always had your humanity. If you didn't have it, you never would've helped me."

"I guess so." He kissed her. She renewed him and soothed his soul. He'd become a better man because of her. "Babe, you're trembling."

"I'm cold." Jessica shivered. "Wish I had that jacket." She stared at him. "But I can't put my wings away." Her eyes widened. "Something is wrong. Lane?"

He'd seen this before. The death of a demon changed everything the demon touched. She could die. Did other demons have children? Would the demon genes within her die, too? Humans possessed by demons returned to their human form when the demon died. But she wasn't fully demonic or fully fae. "Hestia."

Jessica shuddered. "I'm cold." She clung to him. "I don't want to die."

"I know, baby." He held her closer. "Hestia." He needed the stronger faerie's help. "We can't fix this without you."

"Ma's not coming." Jessica shivered. "We need to throw his body into a portal to Hades."

Lane opened his palm and murmured the words to a portal spell. Unlike every other time, nothing happened. What the...? He spoke the words again. Still nothing. He checked his palm. The pentagram was gone. "Shit. Jess, I can't."

"What?" Her color returned. She still leaned into him, but held herself up. "You're a demon."

"Not any longer." He showed her his palm. "It's gone. I'm not marked."

She caressed his hand. "I cured you." She met his gaze. "What about me?"

He turned her palm over. The pentagram had been etched into her skin. "You can do it. Repeat what I say and hold out your hands. I'll help you open the portal."

She pressed her back into his chest and tugged his arms around her. Her wings dipped, allowing him to rest his chin on her shoulder. Although he spoke the words, her voice came out strong and clear. "*Tegeddot munoos domina desposito eren.*"

Just as he'd expected, fire flew from her hands and the portal opened beneath Nicco's corpse.

"No one needs this trash." She held up both hands. Flames shot from her fingertips and she forced Nicco into the portal. Fireworks spiraled in his wake. Sparks blasted toward the sky.

Lane clung to Jessica. He couldn't lose her and refused to let go in case Nicco tried one last time to kill her. He yanked her hands down, closing the portal.

Jessica sagged into him and both collapsed onto the tiles. "Holy shit."

"Yeah." He held her. "That was intense."

Jessica was still paled, but her hair and eyes were vibrant again. Her wings were still dark and now had scorch marks. She held out her hand. The pentagram remained. "I'm a monster," she whispered.

"No." He turned her around in his arms. "You're not."

"I'm a demaerie? Faemon?" She frowned. "I'm a mess."

"You're an original." He cupped her jaw. "A faerie with special capabilities. You're amazing."

She blushed, reminding him of a porcelain doll. "Lane."

"Now you're embarrassed?" He kissed her. "I'm honored to know you. That, and I'm proud. You destroyed a demon. Paranormals will be thrilled when they find out. You saved so many lives."

Her smile wavered. "Ma's dead."

"What?" He had to have heard her wrong. "What do you mean?"

"She's dead. Instead of coming back to this realm, she's decided to stay in Hades with Duke. She refused to leave him." Jessica cried again. "I lost her and my father all in one day."

"What does her being gone mean?"

"I'm in charge." She froze. "I'm not good at being in charge. That's why I ran the bar and hid my talents."

"Stop." He brushed his thumb across her bottom lip. "You beat a demon. That's huge. Then you saved my rotten ass. I didn't think that was possible. If your mother felt she needed to stay with Duke in Hades, then she trusted you to take over. She knew you could do this. You've done so much anyway — stuff you never thought you could do."

"Lane." She clutched his shirt sleeves. "I'm scared."

"Of?"

"I'll screw up."

"You've got Cory and Kali."

"Because of me, Jinx was killed."

"Your father did that and you cannot be held responsible," Lane said. "That's on him, not you."

"I didn't stop him fast enough."

"You did what you needed to when it had to be done." He brushed his thumb across her lips again. "Baby, you'll make mistakes. It happens. We all do. But we're a family. You have your cousins. The paranormals will have your back because you're one of them and helped save them all."

"What about you?"

"I'm on your side. Always."

"Take me home." She rested her head on his shoulder and threaded her arm around his waist.

"Your house is destroyed."

"Your penthouse isn't." Her skin was still pale, but the sparkle had returned to her eyes. "You annoyed me, but you've been loyal and aren't acting like a dick now that you're human. I'm stepping way out of my comfort zone and trusting you. Take me home?"

"I'll work hard to be the man you deserve." He kissed her. "Thank you, babe. Let's go downstairs."

"Wait." She grinned. "I got this." She snapped her fingers. Within seconds, she and Lane stood in the living room of his penthouse.

"Whoa." He laughed. "I'll never get used to that."

"You will." She nudged him onto the couch and crawled onto his lap. "I saved you. How about you show your appreciation?"

"Yes, my faerie. My pleasure." He scooped her into his arms and carried her to the bedroom.

* * * *

She wrapped her legs around his waist and held on until he placed her on the bed. "This is the scene of an awful lot of crimes—including ours." She wouldn't change a second for anything. He made her happy and hadn't walked away when things got tough.

"Not a crime." He whipped his shirt off. His nipples beaded and he flexed his muscles, showing off his tattoos. "I loved every moment of what we've done." He paused. "Baby, I don't bring everyone to my bedroom. You're the first.'

"Don't lie. I already like you." He didn't have to smooth this over. He'd won her heart.

He shook his head. "My penthouse has always been my personal space. If anyone saw my ass or walked into my inner sanctum, they'd know I'm not a mage. I didn't want the truth to get out."

"Being a demon isn't awful," she said. She'd seen his human side. "It's not great for your character, but maybe it would've made him more interesting—a demon mage? Or would you get canned if the truth came out?"

"Lots of people wanted to sleep with a handsome mage. Not many want to lay down with a demon." He removed his boots, then opened his pants. "My character made people think of sex. They wanted me."

"Really?" She tucked her legs beneath her. "I don't believe you." She'd never seen the show and while he had charisma...was he really that much of a sex symbol?

"It's what I'm told. You've seen the line of fans at the convention."

"I did." He was magnetic.

"I don't want to talk about my show any longer," he said. "You try to be tough all the time and you keep people at arm's length." He kissed her shoulder and settled behind her. "You're good at tough, but you're good at sweet, too."

Desire flowed through her veins. Her nipples beaded and she leaned into his touch. "Maybe."

He trailed his fingers along her arms and sent shivers down her spine. Lane kissed her shoulder again. "But you don't have to be tough with me." He nipped at the side of her neck. "I love your strength and spirit. Be tough. It's sexy."

She closed her eyes and relaxed. "But?"

"But you can be soft with me." He tugged her shirt from her jeans. "I want to be the man you need—the one who cherishes you and makes you whole."

"Yes." She leaned into him. She needed to be loved. "Want it." She twisted around to face him. "I want you."

"You have me." He abandoned his position

on the bed and knelt between her knees. He removed her boots. "You're gorgeous."

"Even with my scars?" She extended her wings and parted her thighs.

"Everything about you is perfect." He unzipped her jeans, then tugged the denim and her panties down her legs.

Chilly air kissed her lower half. She liked having someone she could bare herself to and not be judged. Her skin sizzled and she bit back a moan as she reclined on the bed.

Lane settled between her knees. "Gorgeous." He parted her pussy lips and nuzzled along her inner thigh.

A wave of excitement washed through her. She propped herself up on her elbows to watch him.

"So wet." He glanced up at her, then closed his eyes. His breath tickled her skin.

She extended her wings and tilted her head back. She couldn't focus. All she could do was feel. He dragged his tongue between the folds of her labia until he sucked on her clit.

She jerked. The explosion of sensation overwhelmed her for a moment. She gritted her teeth. He knew where to touch her to make her crazy. She settled on her back and rubbed her breasts. The twin feelings of desire added to her delight. Magic swirled within her and she bucked against Lane's mouth.

"Beautiful." He sucked hard on her clit until she cried out.

"Lane." She pinched her nipples, then caressed her breasts. He pushed her closer toward orgasm. Her restraint would never hold up. She dug her feet into the mattress and her skin heated. She trembled.

"Good girl." He eased one finger into her cunt and pumped.

The combination of him inside her and on her clit, as well as her hands on her breasts, nearly destroyed her self-control. She rode his finger and moaned.

"Christ, that's gorgeous." He bit her labia. "Let go, baby. Come on me."

The bit of pain nudged her closer to the edge. Her legs trembled and she couldn't breathe. Magic swirled around her. She reached for him and grasped his free hand. Heat from the mark on her palm seared her. She met his gaze. Was he overwhelmed, too?

"Fuck." His skin shimmered red and flames burned in his eyes. His hair darkened and horns sprang from his scalp.

So much for his humanity returning. But did she care? No. She rode his finger and embraced the growing orgasm. He let go of her hand and smoothed his palm over her belly. His nails lengthened into claws and he scratched her. She welcomed the burn.

"Lane." She arched under his touch. One or two more pumps and she'd come apart. She trembled from head to toe and her movements turned jerky. A moan erupted from her throat. She dug her fingers into the bedding as the climax hit at full force. All she could do was hold on. Nothing else mattered—just Lane and the way he made her feel.

"Yes, baby." Lane sucked hard on her clit, adding to her excitement. She closed her eyes and floated. The scent of him lingered in the air and she could still taste his kiss.

"You're glowing." Lane trailed his fingers down her ribs to her groin. "You're the most beautiful shade of red."

She didn't care. She couldn't open her eyes, either. A whimper bubbled within her. She didn't want the moment to end. "Lane." Her power increased and for a second, she could do anything. "Lane?"

"Right here." He crawled on top of her. He fitted his erection between her sensitive pussy lips. Instead of entering her, he rubbed. His hair tickled her cheek as he nibbled on her throat. "My faerie."

She draped her arms around his neck. "My demon." She curled her legs around him. The shift in position pinned his cock between their bodies.

Lane adjusted and pushed to the hilt into her. Instead of beginning to thrust, he held still as she adjusted around him.

The craving within her increased. Her senses returned to full-alert. She writhed beneath him and moaned. Her wings fluttered, despite being partially pinned beneath her. The glow of her skin switched from red to white.

Lane's demon remained at the forefront. He braced himself on his hands and started to thrust. When he bared his teeth, his fangs gleamed. The fires in his eyes intensified.

She rolled her hips and smoothed her hands over his chest. The tattoo over his heart glowed. Every cell in her body sensitized. She couldn't breathe.

"Yes." Lane increased his speed. The springs squeaked beneath their bodies and the sound of his grunts filled the air.

She whimpered. Any words evaporated before she could speak them. When he leaned over her again and kissed her, she sucked on his tongue. She needed every bit of him. The demon might have claimed Lane, but she owned both. She swallowed his moans.

He broke the connection and roared. "Fuck." His lips curled and he tipped his head back. His movements turned feral. "Come with me."

Like she could hold back? She welcomed the release. Her craving couldn't be contained and the coil wound tight in her belly needed sprung. She gasped.

"Yes." Lane pistoned into her and his roar thundered through the room. The veins were visible in his neck and his nails bit into her skin. He pushed to the hilt and his cock throbbed. Once he added a few more thrusts, he slumped over her. His skin returned to his natural color. His horns and claws retracted. The fires dimmed in his eyes until he regained his humanity. He panted and perspiration glistened on his forehead. He panted.

She tugged him to her chest and sighed. Now that she had Lane, she'd never be the simple lone faerie she'd been before. He drew out her sensual side and made her want to be better. Her heart beat in time with his. When she looked into his eyes, she saw forever. She also saw happiness and security. Not only did he love her, but he belonged to her.

"Shit." Lane chucked. "That was supposed to last longer."

"I like frantic." She toyed with the hairs at the base of his skull. "Next time you can go slower. We have the rest of our lives together."

"We do." He eased out of her and settled next to her on the bed. "My demon returned."

"I saw." She rolled onto her side and slid her arm across his chest. "It was sexy."

"The little demon came out of you, too." He draped her across his torso and twined his legs with hers. "I've never seen anything sexier." He closed his eyes and sighed. "I can't stay awake. You wore me out."

"Likewise." She grasped the sheet and dragged it over their bodies. "Rest. We have plenty of time for round two."

"Yes." He relaxed beside her. "We do."

Jessica cuddled in his arms. Within seconds, sleep claimed her. A vision formed in her mind. Where was she? Not in Lane's room any longer. She stumbled on the rocky terrain. Flames shot from cracks at her feet. She glanced down at her attire—at least she was clothed.

"Where am I?" She crinkled her nose. *"Hello?"*

Hestia and Duke stepped out of the fog.

Her heart hammered. *"You're here."* Jessica threw her arms around her mother, then Duke. *"Why...Are you cursed to Hades?"*

"I'm not." Hestia threaded her arm around Duke's. *"I could go."*

"Why stay here?" She wished she could take

the words back as soon as she asked them. *"Duke."*

Her mother nodded.

"I know you love each other, but Ma, I need you."

"We needed each other more," Hestia said. *"You're going to be fine."*

"I can't do this alone. You've put me in charge. I can't take care of myself, let alone solve the problems of any para that comes my way," she said. *"It's your job. You're the powerful faerie. I'm an imposter."*

"You're not serious." Hestia turned Jessica's hand over. *"The demon marked you."*

"I know. Is it bad? He helped me defeat Nicco."

"It's not the end of the world."

She didn't understand. *"Then what's the problem? What's Lane got to do with you being here? He didn't curse you or me. He didn't…kill Duke."*

"Darling, in each faerie's time, he or she learns when to step away. It's mine and you're ready to lead," Hestia said.

"I'm so not ready."

"I let you doubt yourself for too long," Hestia said. *"It's my turn to build you up."*

"Ma, no one respects me. They don't listen and they think I'm a screw-up." She'd been written off years ago.

"You're my daughter. They have plenty of respect and they will have more when they learn the truth — you vanquished a demon."

"I don't know how to lead," Jessica replied. *"I mix drinks and poof stuff into existence."*

"Do you think I knew how to take care of the faeries when I took over? I didn't, but I learned. You will, too. The demon will help, so will Cory and Kali.

You're not alone."

"You actually trust Lane enough to help me?" Jessica asked.

"He's not your father."

"I hope not." Not after what they'd done. She embraced the relief that she wouldn't be alone, but a new wave of queasiness hit. *"I got Jinx killed."*

Hestia shook her head. "Nicco didn't kill him."

"But...I saw him. He died." She clutched her stomach. *"I saw him."*

"You saw a lie. Your father wanted you to think it was the truth so you'd run. After what you saw me go through, he thought he could control you. He tried to get into your head and doubt yourself," Hestia said. *"It almost worked."*

"Almost?" Her voice cracked. *"I did. I thought my friend was dead."*

"He's alive and living it up with Henry. I hear they've gotten married," Hestia said. *"They worked fast."*

"No shit." She wobbled on her feet. He wasn't dead? Good.

"Little girl." Hestia glared at her. "Language."

Jessica shrugged. *"I'm shocked, but I'm glad he's alive."* She paused. *"What about Lane? You don't like him."*

Hestia sighed. *"Lane might be a poor choice by my standards, but he's loyal and loves you. He'll help you. He knows the ways of the demons and will protect you."* She hugged Jessica. *"I have faith in him and mostly you."*

"What if I fail?"

"What if you do? You won't get everything right." Hestia held Duke's singed hand. He still wore the ragged, dirty clothes from the moment he'd died. Blood marred his face, but the sparkle had returned to his eyes. *"We need to go,"* Hestia said. *"We've kept you here for too long."*

"You'd rather die than be with your family?" Jessica asked. She'd been mean, but wasn't ready to lose her mother, too.

"I had what I thought was love and I got you. But that love nearly killed me. Now I have love that's pure. I won't let it go." Hestia laced her fingers with Duke's and smiled. *"You have the same thing with Lane. Embrace it."*

"I – " At least she had her mother's blessing.

"You'll be fine." Hestia kissed Jessica's forehead. *"You chose love for the right reason. Enjoy it."*

"Jess?"

Hestia and Duke faded. Jessica reached for them, but instead plunged into darkness. "Ma?"

"Jess." Lane's voice filtered to her. "Babe?" He jostled her shoulder. "Wake up."

She blinked. The dream was over and she'd returned to the bedroom with Lane. Her mother and Duke were back in Hades. "It's true."

"What, babe?" Lane tucked her to his side. "Tell me."

"Ma's staying in Hades with Duke. I'm in charge." She expected to cry, but no tears came. "She said I needed to be happy and lead." An odd sense of relief washed over her. "She thinks I can do this."

"Congrats?" He held her. "And I'm sorry?"

"Don't be sorry." She cupped his cheek. "I'm okay with it." Everyone had a course in life and she had to follow hers while being happy. Lane made her whole. For the first time in years, she wasn't afraid of the future. "She said to be with you."

"I'm not leaving, so that's good." He brushed her hair from her eyes. "I've got you."

"I know." He'd give her strength and anything else she wanted. She had a partner in Lane. "I'm the head cheese, which makes you the second cheese in command."

"That's a lot of cheese." He chuckled. "Are you sure? I'm positive you've got this."

"I fought two demons and won versus both." Holy shit. Had any other faerie done that? She figured so and wanted to know who because they'd get a frickin' medal.

"You've disarmed me, yes, but it wasn't much of a contest." His smile widened. "Sweetheart, I would've given in no matter what."

"And Nicco…I caused…" She sighed, not wanting to say the words *his death* out loud. Time to move and look forward, not back. "I'm happy and I'm not scared any longer. If I mess up, I do." She nodded. "You're willing to be with me even though I'm in charge. That's sexy."

"Boss lady, you're too hot to let go of and I'm kind of in love with you, so I'm good and staying put," Lane said.

"You're done acting?"

"Completely."

"This kind of makes us like a king and queen…" She frowned. "Queen and king?"

"It makes us *us*." He kissed her. "I love you, Jess. I don't care what your title is as long as you're mine."

"I love you, too, Lane." She'd never be the most conventional faerie. She wore boots and black instead of sparkles and pastels. She liked loud music, not nature sounds, but she cared. The faeries and paranormals needed her. She had the love of her life—with a man who loved her along with her scars—and a purpose. She had her best life ever and now her happy ever after, too.

ABOUT THE AUTHOR

Megan Slayer is a multi-published, award-winning author of more than one-hundred short stories and novels. She's been writing since 2008 and published since 2009. Her stories range from the contemporary and paranormal to BDSM and LGBTQ themes. No matter what the length, her works are always hot, but with a lot of heart. She enjoys giving her characters a second chance at love, no matter what the form. She's been the runner up in the Kink Category at Love Romances Café as well as nominated at the LRC for best contemporary, best ménage and best anthology. Her books have made it to the bestseller lists on Amazon.com and the former AllRomance Ebooks. She also writes under the name of Wendi Zwaduk.

When she's not writing, she spends time with her husband and son as well as three dogs and three cats. She enjoys art, music and racing, but football is her sport of choice. Find out more about Wendi at: https://www.wendizwaduk.comhttp://www.wendizwaduk.com/ or on her blog: https://wendizwaduk.wordpress.com/

Find her on Facebook, Twitter, Instagram, Bookbub, Goodreads and Amazon.

Other Books by Megan Slayer in the *After Dark Series:*

Faerie Matchmaker
Biting Love
Ariadne's Vampire

Find these and other Megan Slayer titles where ebooks and print books are sold.

FAERIE MATCHMAKER
BY MEGAN SLAYER
BOOK 1 IN THE AFTER DARK SERIES

What's a love faerie supposed to do without her magic?

Cordelia likes to play fast and loose with the rules. So she's made a few mistakes with magic along the way? No one got hurt…right? The blue-haired faerie, prone to the occasional blue language and dirty jokes, loses her right to create magic after one goof-up too many.

But she's about to find redemption in the form of a merman named Henry and a human named Jinx. Fix them up and she'll get her right to create magic back. There's only one problem…Liam.

Liam could be the right man to help Cordelia rise above her troubles…but first she's got to make him believe she exists. Not impossible, right?

BITING LOVE
BY MEGAN SLAYER
BOOK 2 IN THE AFTER DARK SERIES

Mix one vampire with one human who doesn't believe in the paranormal and add some sizzle.

Anson wasn't looking for a partner when he spotted the handsome human, but he's not about to argue when the mood strikes. He's got to bring a date to the Halloween bash and Parker fits his bill exactly. Now all he needs to do is convince Parker that vampires truly exist.

Parker is practical, intelligent and a little on the geeky side. He can't believe his eyes — a handsome man has not only hit on him, but asked him out…to a masquerade ball. He doesn't believe in vampires, but Anson wears his Dracula costume a bit too well.

Can these two find love and trust after all or will the sparks only last until the dawn?

Available wherever ebooks are sold and now in print!

ARIADNE'S VAMPIRE
BY MEGAN SLAYER
BOOK 3 IN THE AFTER DARK SERIES

Available wherever ebooks are sold and now in print!

Ariadne defied her father for love, only to be abandoned. She married for what she thought was love, only to have Dionysus leave her for another woman. Even Aphrodite won't smile on her because Aphrodite wants Dionysus. Ari can't seem to win. What's a goddess to do if she wants love? Find a vampire.

Caden, a vampire and creature of the night, gave up on love long ago. Draining victims, sex and sleep are his orders for each evening…until he's tasked with tracking Ariadne. He doesn't expect the goddess to call to his wounded soul in ways he thought long since dead.

Can a vampire and goddess go the distance or will their happy ending die with the dawn?

Look for the next book in the *After Dark* series in 2020!